TO

The trip to the Yukon had seemed like a gift from heaven, but Aurora rapidly found she had underestimated both the Canadian wilderness and her rugged guide, Chance Cody. Could she cope—with either of them?

TO TAME A WILD HEART

BY
QUINN WILDER

MILLS & BOON LIMITED
15–16 BROOK'S MEWS
LONDON W1A 1DR

All the characters in this book have no existence outside the imagination of the Author, and have no relation whatsoever to anyone bearing the same name or names. They are not even distantly inspired by any individual known or unknown to the Author, and all the incidents are pure invention.

The text of this publication or any part thereof may not be reproduced or transmitted in any form or by any means, electronic or mechanical, including photocopying, recording, storage in an information retrieval system, or otherwise, without the written permission of the publisher.

This book is sold subject to the condition that it shall not, by way of trade or otherwise, be lent, resold, hired out or otherwise circulated without the prior consent of the publisher in any form of binding or cover other than that in which it is published and without a similar condition including this condition being imposed on the subsequent purchaser.

*First published in Great Britain 1987
by Mills & Boon Limited*

© Quinn Wilder 1987

*Australian copyright 1987
Philippine copyright 1987
This edition 1987*

ISBN 0 263 75696 3

*Set in Baskerville 10½ on 11¾ pt.
01-0687-41442*

*Computer typeset by SB Datagraphics,
Colchester, Essex*

*Printed and bound in Great Britain by
Collins, Glasgow*

CHAPTER ONE

'I AM NOT marrying Douglas Hartman.'

The stubborn statement—made with contrived casualness—was quite unrelated to the subdued small talk at the dinner table. Having said what was on her mind, Aurora Fairhurst, with apparent unconcern, popped another delicate bite of braised Cornish game hen into her mouth and secretly delighted in the sensation she had caused. The inbred reserve of her mother and father—for once—seemed to have fled them. Aurora peeped up from her plate, looked down the long stretch of the highly polished mahogany table, and smiled blandly at the stunned expressions, and forks frozen in mid-air.

Her mother's mouth worked soundlessly, until finally a long and plaintive moan emerged. 'Aurora ... you can't possibly mean that! The wedding is only two weeks away ... the invitations are back ... two hundred and fifty confirmed! The cathedral is booked, Sebastian has the menu planned, and I finally was able to get Pierre La Trevaille to do the photography. Darling, he *never* does weddings!' She looked pleadingly at her daughter, and gave a dismayed squawk at the stubborn set of the very faintly clefted jaw. 'Aurora, don't do this to me! What will everybody say?' she wailed with near panic.

Diamond sparks began to spit from slightly narrowed emerald green eyes, and Edna Fairhurst sensed she had taken the wrong tack, though the right tack at the moment eluded her. She shut her mouth with a snap, and turned pleading eyes to the head of the table.

'Very funny, Aurora,' Franklin Fairhurst intoned drily, the cast of his facial features clearly stating that he did not find Aurora's announcement in the least amusing. 'Now stop it, you're upsetting your mother.'

Aurora tossed her heavy mane of shoulder-length auburn hair, and the predominant red strands caught the reflection of muted light from the chandelier and danced a warning of a spirited temperament. She lifted her nose—slender and well-shaped, and turned up a touch at the end—just enough so that she could gaze down it at her father. A perfectly shaped eyebrow arched upwards, and a faint, challenging smile appeared on her lips.

Aurora Fairhurst was not, by a long chalk, heart-stoppingly beautiful, though her large green eyes and fiery hair made her attractive. Add to that years of practice with make-up, and with just the right gesture, lift of the chin, and quirk of the mouth, and she could be considered quite striking. She had to do constant battle with the freckles over her nose and the almost elfin cast of her face, though, to win the accolades 'chic' or 'sophisticated' which had been much sought after descriptions at the Swiss finishing school she had attended.

'Daddy, dear, I am not joking.' Aurora's tone dripped with sweetness and she batted the long tangle of mascara-darkened eyelashes innocently at him.

The bored indulgence left Franklin Fairhurst's face, and a mouth very like his daughter's tautened into a firm line. 'Shall I tell you the facts of life?' he asked in a hard, smooth voice. His face had a ruthless set to it that his business acquaintances were more familiar with than his family, and Aurora contained a surprised shiver of apprehension.

'By all means,' she responded airily, not letting her sudden trepidation show in her face or her tone.

'Fact one,' he said in a clipped voice, devoid of emotion. 'You have been engaged to Douglas for long enough that if you had objections you should have voiced them before now. The embarrassment to your mother at this point is unthinkable—not to mention the heyday the press would have at the expense of the family name.

'Fact two, you have developed a rather insatiable appetite for pretty clothes, baubles, sports cars and travel. Very few men of an acceptable age, and of an acceptable social standing, would be able to satisfy your whims. Douglas can continue to pamper you in the manner to which you are accustomed.

'Fact three——'

'Fact three——' Aurora cut him off, a trace of anger entering her well-modulated tone. '—Daddy and Douglas have many interests in common—very profitable interests that would benefit immensely from the joining of the names Fairhurst and Hartman. And fact four, I ... don't ... love ... Douglas ... Hartman!'

Franklin Fairhurst's eyes had narrowed to beady slits, and a tight, almost cruel smile played across his lips. 'Let's quit playing this game, shall we, and get right to the bottom line? For twenty-two years I have indulged your every whim. You do not have an inkling what it is to want something and not have it. But there is a grim reality that you are long overdue to learn, and it is this: there is a price for everything, and I am calling in my debts.'

'Pardon me!' Aurora exclaimed, hiding in her tone the fact that she felt very shaken. 'I didn't realise there was a price to be paid for being your daughter!' For the first time the horrible possibility occurred to her that perhaps she couldn't talk her way out of marrying Douglas. Her demands had always been met without more than token resistance, and the rock-hard surface she was hitting up against now brought on a wave of concealed panic.

For all the indulgence, Aurora thought, eyeing her father warily, she was under no illusions about love. Giving her everything she wanted was simply easier than giving in to a child's natural demands for attention and genuine affection. Both her parents had always been too busy for that—too wrapped up in their own worlds to bother much with their only child. Parenting was a dull and somewhat mystifying occupation in comparison to the glitter of balls, and the challenges of big business.

Aurora had been shunted off to her first boarding school at the age of six. Her visits home had lost their novelty after one or two paradings before her parents' social circle—a hired companion and a new pony waited somewhere in the wings to whisk her off at the first sign of her mother's flagging interest. Her father was rarely seen. When he was present, his young daughter could count on a pat on the head, time to recount exactly one tale, a peck on the cheek and a promise of a gift. The extravagant, wonderful gifts never quite took away the sting—and now she was being told they had to be paid for!

The first time Aurora could recall genuine interest in her father's eyes was when she had come home from school in Switzerland. She had been bejewelled, expertly made-up, and dressed in designer clothes from jaunts to Italy and France. It had been written clearly in his face that Franklin Fairhurst had just discovered he had a new commodity to deal in.

Aurora didn't know if her father had always been a cold and emotionless man who tended to deal with people in terms of their value to him. But if he had ever been moved by such things as love and passion, that day was long since passed. Empires like the Fairhurst Corporation were not built with tender-hearted emotionalism. Though the famous Fairhurst fortune contained more money than ten families could spend in a lifetime, her father was relentless in his pursuit of more.

Looking at him now, Aurora realised she was looking at a man who was obsessed with the playing of a life-size Monopoly game. Long ago Aurora had realised that her mother was just a playing piece in Franklin Fairhurst's giant board game, someone to manipulate to his best advantage, to use to his greatest gain. Now, with a start, and a creeping sensation of fear, she realised she was no different. His own marriage had been based on mutual benefit to two very strong old families, and the same sacrifice was expected of her. Why hadn't she seen just how much the joining of the Fairhurst and Hartman names had come to mean to that analytical and businesslike mind?

'You can't force me to marry Douglas,' she whispered, and there was nothing artificial in the trembling of her voice.

'Don't bore me with melodrama, Aurora. We've had this conversation before.' He took in her puzzled expression with satisfaction, and then smiled slowly and without warmth. 'Only before it was reversed. Before you were telling me I couldn't force you *not* to marry that dim-witted ski instructor.'

Aurora shut her eyes against the sudden pain that threatened to nauseate her. Sven, she thought; lovely, lovely Sven who had sold himself for a few pieces of silver; admitted—with only a touch of apology in those clear, sky-blue eyes—that it had never really been her. It had been the money. The damned Fairhurst fortune. Sven's betrayal had totally unseated her, left her suspicious of men, and frightened of herself. How could she have been so lacking in discernment? Why hadn't she detected his insincerity? Nothing had shattered her self-confidence as much as loving and trusting a man with her whole heart and soul, only to discover she had been fooled—and made a fool. How could she ever trust herself again?

A year later she had come home from Switzerland. Her friends had managed, even under Madame Lasard's sharp, protective eye, to experiment with sexuality. Aurora had not. Could not. She was deathly afraid of giving her love again, and secretly old-fashioned enough to wonder how you could do *that* without love. Instead she had sharpened the responses that frightened men away, and protected her heart from them. She had retreated behind a well-practised mask that revealed none of her self-doubts, none of her fears, none of her feelings.

She had been introduced to Douglas almost immediately on returning home. He was a slender, incredibly handsome man with brilliant, almost golden eyes, a quick smile, and a suave charm that won both her mother's and her girlfriends' oohing admiration. Douglas was definitely a 'catch'. Still stinging from Sven, still doubting her own judgment in all matters concerning the opposite sex, and still feeling cynical about the very existence of 'love', Aurora had allowed herself docilely—and with a certain sense of relief—to accept Douglas's and her father's plans for her. The relationship, after six months, had proved comfortable, if not sizzling, and Aurora had accepted Douglas's proposal of marriage with something closer to resignation than excitement. At least, she had thought diplomatically, Douglas wasn't using her.

It wasn't that she didn't like Douglas. She liked him just fine. He was courteous, decent, solid, respectable. He was only mildly disapproving of her lapses of temper and the tendency to mischievousness that had made her so heartily unpopular with her teachers at school.

Aurora wasn't even sure she wouldn't marry Douglas one day. She just didn't want that day to be two weeks hence. Her unease with her engagement had started several months ago. The reasons for the unease were evasive and foggy, and she'd tried to suppress the feeling altogether. But as the day grew closer the vague feeling grew more urgent.

She couldn't pinpoint what it was exactly. An odd aching in her when she listened to a tender love song, or caught the way two lovers looked at each other with long and lingering wonder. An almost suffocating sense of missing something that was integral to the human experience ... a crushing sense of selling a part of herself that she'd never get back once it was gone.

She recognised, at an intuitive level, that the gaping wound left by Sven was closing and healing, and that safety and security were losing their appeal.

In fact, the safe and comfortable life she could look forward to with Douglas—her future—sometimes seemed to be unfolding before her eyes in an unending line of boredom. And boredom suddenly seemed more frightening than risk. Year upon year of sameness, of doing much what she had been doing for the past year. Establishing herself as a power to contend with, just as her mother was. Working for charity committees and the opera society and hosting galas. Keeping busy, and yet never quite believing in the issues, and sensing a yawning emptiness opening up beneath the hectic schedule and the frantic daily pace.

She fought it. Fought acknowledging that she was bored and restless and not the least bit interested in living out yet another version of her mother's life: attending benefit balls and sitting on opera committees, playing tennis on Thursdays, bridge on Fridays, and spending monotonous weekends at the country club lying around the pool, or pretending to enjoy golf.

She fought it because what she really wanted seemed immature and naïve and unrealistic and romantic. Aurora Fairhurst wanted an adventure. She wanted to get up in the morning and not know what the next twenty-four hours held for her. She wanted to feel some challenge, some meaning in her life, some magic. She wanted—just once—to dance with life. To laugh and to live and to explore some of all that wonderful mystery she sensed in the world. She wanted to explore herself—her potentials, her strengths, her weaknesses, the sides of her nature that convention left repressed and unsatisfied and of which her father and Douglas would disapprove heartily.

Marriage and Douglas, she finally acknowledged, were not going to spring her from the trap, but mire her hopelessly in a dull, listless, laughterless life that would eventually make her into a hollow-eyed shadow like her mother.

Finally, she couldn't run from her unease any longer; Aurora recognised that a part of her was going to die undiscovered if she gave in and married Douglas.

And so, striving to look casual and composed and unconcerned, she made her announcement to her parents. Certainly she had expected a protest from her family—and had expected she would have no problem tantruming her way out of it. But looking into Franklin Fairhurst's face now, she knew she had underestimated the stakes he was playing for. She felt a wave of desperation, and wildly entertained plans of cleaning out her bank account and running away. How long, she wondered weakly, could a person live on five thousand dollars? Good heavens, she had paid more than that for her Dior wedding gown!

Her father was shrewd at guessing thoughts before they were spoken, and he interrupted her mental meanderings now.

'Don't even think of it, Aurora,' he said, an icy threat

barely concealed in his cultured voice. 'There's nowhere for you to go where I can't find you. And be realistic—even if you could go somewhere, what on earth could you do? Your rather dismal showing at school has left you unqualified to be much other than the delightful wife of a wealthy man. You couldn't survive for a week trying to look after yourself.'

He had just very succinctly articulated her own doubts, and she felt the trap closing around her. For the first time she chastised herself for her rebellious efforts to win her parents' attention that accounted for the 'dismal' showing her father had just referred to.

'May I please be excused?' she asked haughtily, praying that the dizzy, horrified sensation at the pit of her stomach couldn't be seen.

'Certainly,' her father rejoined with mock courtesy.

Edna Fairhurst looked anxiously between her daughter and her husband. 'Is the wedding on?' she asked worriedly.

'Of course,' Mr Fairhurst assured her suavely, casting a challenging glance at Aurora. 'Just a small case of pre-nuptial nerves.'

Was it just pre-nuptial nerves? Aurora lay on her back on her ridiculously large bed. She bounced her head up and down once or twice, imagining that her hair was cascading in a wild and sexy design across the silk-encased pillow. She soon grew bored with the activity and reminded herself crossly that she had not the faintest idea what *was* wild and sexy, and then, weakly, that she was probably never going to find out. She looked down at the sensuous curve of her bosom and studied and stretched each of her long limbs in turn. Wasted, she thought grimly. Douglas never seemed to notice that she even had a bosom. She wondered, dully, if she was even a little bit sexy. Not if Douglas's reactions—or, more appropriately, his lack of them—counted for anything. Occasionally she noted an admiring look from a man, but she tended to be very suspicious of admiring looks from men. How could she know if the looks were honest or if most men were complete sycophants, just like Sven had been?

For a moment the crushing fear, the panicky trapped feeling she had experienced right after dinner, returned, but she pushed it determinedly away, and a slow fury began to boil inside her.

They couldn't make her! For heaven's sake, it was the twentieth century. Nobody forced people to get married any more. She wasn't some disgustingly faint-witted Victorian wallflower after all! Her father couldn't force her to marry someone she didn't want to marry—could he?

She needed time, she thought desperately. Time away from the influences of her family and her friends and Douglas, to sort out what *she* really wanted. Time to figure out if her yearning for that elusive 'something' was rational and realistic, or just a foolish romantic notion. She sighed. Her prospects of postponing the wedding, instead of calling it off completely, seemed slight. How, she wondered blackly, does one go about catching pneumonia?

'What?' she responded irritably to the soft rap on her door.

'Telephone, Miss Aurora,' the muted voice replied.

'I'm not speaking to anyone right now,' she declared coldly.

'Yes, miss. It's Miss Melinda, and she said it was very important, but perhaps——'

Aurora considered. Of all her friends, she probably liked Melinda—Mindy—Harrison the best. Mindy had it, she thought sourly: had that wonderful *joie de vivre* and that 'I'm grabbing life by the horns' attitude that nobody else she knew quite had. Good old Mindy, who, much to the dismay of Madame Lasard, had managed to get herself involved in the very unfeminine and dangerous sport of mountaineering. Good old Mindy, who was her only friend who hadn't been completely taken with Douglas—in fact disliked him to the point where she had made other plans for the weekend of the wedding.

'I'll talk to her,' Aurora called, and plugged in the phone beside her bed. 'Hi, Mindy. How's life?'

'I've got problems, love,' Mindy said, missing Aurora's forlorn tone completely. 'Big problems.'

Must be catching, Aurora thought, without a great deal of sympathy. At that moment she suspected Mindy didn't know what a real problem was.

'Aurora, I'm all signed up for a trip to the Yukon, and I can't possibly go. Not possibly. I met the most devastating man and he's invited me to spend a month at his villa in Monte Carlo. It's all above board—which isn't preventing Mums from having a fit—but I'm devastated about missing the Yukon trip.'

Aurora stifled a yawn. 'Where's the Yukon?'

'Darling! Are you serious?' Mindy laughed at Aurora's silence. 'You're serious. It's in northern Canada. Over two hundred thousand miles of pristine, barely touched wilderness——'

'Yuk,' Aurora interrupted.

'Twice the size of England, and you don't even know it exists?'

'Shoot me,' Aurora suggested drily.

'Can't. I need you. The trip is really pricy, Aurora. I mean really. There's a guy who works at Miller's—that's the outdoors shop on Fifth—who is just a sweetie. Miller's isn't open right now, and I won't have time to pop over in the morning, so a small favour? Could you run down there and give Davie the info? He'd love to go, and he'd never be able to afford it—like not in a million years. Get this, Aurora, they fly you in by helicopter, and drop you off, and like you're walking where no man has ever set foot before. Hardly, anyway. Two weeks, and no turning back. Like I'm talking total isolation and self-reliance . . .'

A light snapped on in Aurora's dark tunnel of despair and her hand tightened on the receiver. 'When?' she demanded, almost fearful of the thought that had leapt into her mind.

'Starting Monday after this, and going until the sixteenth. Aurora, I told you all about this—it was my perfect excuse not to be at your wedding, remember? But now I have an even better one. His name is Ken and . . .'

Aurora could hardly hear her friend for the hope that had begun to pound noisily in her chest. The wedding would come and go—and even Papa would be hard pressed to find her in two hundred thousand miles of wilderness. Time. It would buy her that precious time.

'Are you listening?' Mindy asked, and Aurora forced

her attention back to her friend, and tried to listen very carefully.

'This is what you have to tell Davie. It's an experience-only expedition, and, like, they mean it. I was tested. I got an application form and then a questionnaire, and then Mr Chance Cody phoned me himself. Tell Davie to call him and OK the switch. It won't be any problem. Davie has a whole lot more experience and expertise than me. But I have the feeling Chance doesn't like surprises. And no wonder! When you're a million miles from anywhere, and the helicopter's gone, you don't need surprises. And I have a feeling you don't need Chance Cody mad at you. Sexy voice, really sexy, but a kind of steely no-nonsense note running through it. I bet he's seven feet tall and has a beard. Did you get all that?'

'Seven feet tall and has a beard,' Aurora repeated obediently. And I'm not afraid of Chance Cody, she added dramatically to herself—not when my whole life is at stake.

'I'll drop you by an envelope tonight. It's got the equipment list, the helicopter chit, and some other info in it. If you can just run it over to Miller's for me tomorrow, and impress upon Davie that he's got to call Chance first—that's really important.'

'I got that part,' Aurora said, striving to sound casual and uninterested. 'See you in a bit.' She hung up the phone, and looked with surprise at her shaking hands.

Her hands felt as if they were still shaking as she glanced down at the young man lacing up her hiking boots.

'Take a little walk,' Davie Johnson suggested, giving

the boot a final slap, and standing up.

'No pinching?'

Aurora shook her head. Davie frowned at the boots. 'They're a good all-round hiking boot—nice and light, good flexible sole—but I'd feel better if you could tell me just a bit more about the terrain.'

Aurora glanced at him sharply. Suspicious? No, she decided. Why on earth would he be suspicious? The plane ticket in her purse, made out to I C Freedom, was making her paranoid. She looked at the growing heap of equipment by the cash register. It was all becoming rather irrevocable. She shuddered, felt Davie's curious eyes on her, and forced a smile. Of course he'd be a little curious that such an obvious novice was gearing up so extensively. For the most part, though, he was keeping his curiosity to himself, and she was finding his expertise reassuring.

Something he said registered and she came back to the present with a thud.

'Bears?' she echoed with ill-concealed panic.

'One of the last domains of the great grizzly,' he told her with nauseating enthusiasm.

She paled before his eyes, and he reassured her hastily, obviously seeing his gigantic sale slipping away.

'Look, I've never used them, but a friend of mine swears by mothballs. He says the odour is repugnant to bears. If you scatter them around the camp, they'll cover up more enticing smells and keep the bears at bay.'

I'm not going, she told herself, tuning Davie out. I can't! Bears! She abruptly took hold of herself.

Come on, Aurora, she sneered, you've been longing for an adventure! You've been yearning to break out of the boring routines and do something challenging and daring. For once in your life, kid, she encouraged herself, take a risk, step out of the mould, and into the unknown.

'You probably won't even see a bear.'

Aurora forced herself to see his words as a guarantee. She had to go!

Even if the trip was an absolute horror, which it well might be, it would serve its purpose. It would keep her away from her own wedding, well out of even Franklin Fairhurst's long reach, and well away from the daily pressures that she suspected might wear her down to a point where she would capitulate to the loveless match with Douglas.

So what if she had to sacrifice two weeks to buy the time to know her own mind, to show her father she wasn't to be manipulated like a puppet on his string? Douglas wouldn't be happy about any of this but, if she decided she did want to marry him after all, she was confident he'd forgive her and have her back. And if she decided she couldn't marry him, she had better figure out how to support herself, because her father was sure to disown her.

'Personally, I think this is the best tent ever made. Four and a half pounds——'

'Fine. I'll take it.' She felt only the briefest stab of guilt for depriving this earnest young man of the trip that should rightfully have been his. His commission on the sales he was making would more than make up for it, she assured herself.

Aurora boarded the helicopter and gave her fellow passengers only the most cursory of glances. She noted two freckle-faced young men who must have been twins, and a girl a little older than herself, dark-haired and attractive in a raw outdoorsy fashion. Aurora dismissed her fellow adventurers as being a rather dull and uninteresting lot, and opened a thick copy of *Glamour*, immersing herself in it rather than looking out of the windows. On the plane to Whitehorse yesterday she had begun to understand the immensity of this land, and had found the miles and miles of unbroken bush and hills and mountain ranges to be more than a little intimidating. Now, she refused to so much as glance out of the window, afraid that the almost crushing sense of isolation that she had experienced yesterday would return. Far better to immerse herself in the familiar pages of a fashion magazine.

She was aware that her fellow passengers were regarding her with far more interest than she had allowed them, and she even thought she detected faint puzzlement—as if it were blatantly obvious that she were out of place on this trip. Impossible, she told herself; she looked just like one of them. Davie had outfitted her in the proper clothing as well as gear, and Aurora was clad in a checked wool shirt—that would have gagged her mother, she thought with satisfaction—and a pair of sturdy hiking trousers with several buckled pockets. When Aurora had regarded her appearance this morning in the full-length mirror in her Whitehorse hotel room she had laughed out loud with devilish delight. Goodness, this was as much fun as dressing up for a fancy dress ball!

In fact, this morning it had all seemed like such fun. She had thoroughly enjoyed the subterfuge of travelling incognito, and changing planes several times more than it was necessary to throw her father off her trail. This morning she had felt a wonderful sense of triumph for thwarting the tentacles of the Fairhurst Corporation successfully. In a few more minutes she would be totally out of reach.

Except it didn't feel fun now. Now there seemed to be something terribly irrevocable about it all. The knot in her stomach tightened, and she suppressed a small shiver.

Why are you nervous? she demanded of herself, and her gaze drifted, almost unwillingly, out of the window. Her heart fell with a thud. Had she lost her mind? There was nothing out here—unless she counted a billion trees that all looked the same. She bit back a nervous giggle. She still had the seven-foot bearded giant who didn't like surprises to contend with. Well, Chance Cody had his money, besides which she had no intention of letting on that she wasn't Mindy. If it became evident a few days down the road that she was a little inexperienced, so what? He'd been paid.

The helicopter began to drop down, and Aurora furiously fought her nerves, making a relieved note that there didn't seem to be anything intimidating about the clearing they were landing in.

What followed was general confusion as Aurora struggled to remember the briefing the pilot had given them about safely exiting from his machine. She got herself and her pack off in one piece, and crouched on the ground, hands over her ears. She was vaguely aware that a wiry blond youth now stood on the fringes of the group, counting heads and greeting people, but she was far more aware of using every bit of discipline she possessed not to run and jump back on the helicopter before it departed and left her here in this brooding wilderness with four people she didn't know.

The young blond gave the chopper pilot a thumbs up sign, and it lifted back into the sky like a great awkward bird. Aurora uncovered her ears, and rose, watching her only link with civilisation leaving with unveiled wistfulness in her eyes. She was beginning, too late, to seriously doubt the sanity of the impulse that had landed her in the middle of the Canadian wilderness. She glanced around almost warily, seeing only forbidding walls of pines on all sides of the clearing.

She shifted her attention quickly to the guide to avoid the stifling effect of too many soaring trees. Was he Chance Cody? He was young and skinny, not seven feet tall, and not in the least bit steely, though there seemed to be a faint hostility about him.

A movement seen from the corner of her eyes drew Aurora's gaze back to the line of trees and her breath caught in her throat. Another man was breaking from the forest and coming toward them.

He was very tall—probably an inch or two over six feet—and very broad across the shoulders. He wore a wool plaid shirt, rolled up neatly past the rippling muscles in his arms, and a pair of faded khaki hiking slacks that emphasised the lean, long line of his leg, and the corded muscle of his thigh. For a big man he walked with awesome grace, something almost animal in the fluid, powerful motion of his body. Though he carried a large expedition pack he walked effortlessly, and Aurora found herself thinking of an unencumbered panther moving on sure, silent feet.

As he drew closer, her attention moved from the spellbinding ease of his movement to his face, and again Aurora had to fight a gasp, though of awe or dismay she couldn't be sure.

The man had the most arresting face she had ever seen. He was not handsome, or at least not Hollywood handsome like Douglas was—his face was far too strong to be called attractive by the traditional definition of that word. There was a hint of Indian in him, the blood of some fierce and faraway ancestor emerging in the hawk-like hook of his nose, in the high jutting cheekbones, as rugged and sharp as rock-faces. His skin was the colour of burnished bronze, his lips set in a proud line, that pride re-emphasised in the almost haughty tilt of a strong, square jaw. His eyes were jet black, hard and glittering as obsidian, a diamond spark glinting in them with what could equally have been savagery or mocking amusement of mere mortals. His hair was black and fine, shining with brilliant highlights under the morning sun, and, though it was cut short, Aurora could see a hint of curl beginning to turn up impertinently at the tips.

But if he was attractive at all, Aurora thought—and she was not at all convinced that he was—the attraction lay deeper than the arresting grace of his stride, the power of his physique, the strength of his face. He radiated something almost electrical—a pure animal magnetism, an unmistakable and rugged virility, a raw strength so intense it was frightening to a girl accustomed to men like her father and Douglas, men who oozed refinement and culture and polish.

His casual stance, his clothing—that differed not

much from her own—did nothing to hide the fact that there was something faintly feral about this man. A quality of fierceness, of independence, of self-reliance broke through the thin trappings of his exterior garments. He held his head at an angle that both challenged and mocked the world that might have tried to tame him. Aurora felt certain a man stood before her who belonged to no one, the only claim on his heart that of the harsh wilderness all around them, a man who had made his own rules, and lived by them. For some reason the thought made her shiver, and made her even more uncertain whether this powerful specimen of manhood repelled or attracted her.

There was no need for a formal explanation that this man was the expedition leader, and without prodding the group naturally drifted towards him, forming an expectant semi-circle around him.

'I'm Chance Cody,' he introduced himself. His voice was deep, vibrant and sensual. He had no need to raise it when he addressed the group—a hush had fallen as soon as he began to speak.

A faint, slightly mocking smile played across his lips, revealing straight, perfect teeth that looked almost impossibly white against the bronze of his skin. 'I could swear I smell Shalimar,' Chance Cody commented lightly, and the group responded with laughter that was lost on Aurora.

'The question is, who's wearing it?'

Aurora, who had been seeking refuge behind one of the twins' backs for a reason she hardly knew, didn't know what to say. She was wearing the fragrance, but she was also busy digesting the information that this man could pick up the faintest whiff of perfume, confirming the fact for her that he operated by some baser instinct. To smell the perfume was one thing—to identify the expensive scent proclaimed a rather unsettling knowledge about women.

Chance Cody didn't continue, obviously waiting for the perfume wearer to own up, giving Aurora the uneasy feeling a minor crime had been committed. And even though his voice had been pleasant, and even amused, Aurora didn't miss the subtle disapproving crease around his mouth. She wanted to shrink back and disappear, but the eyes suddenly found her and rested on her, accusing her mockingly of hiding.

Defiantly she stepped away from the back that had been shielding her. 'I'm wearing Shalimar,' she conceded with a toss of her shimmering hair that asked no forgiveness.

Yet she almost staggered under the impact of that raking glance. The frown around that firm mouth deepened as the eyes assessed her, and Aurora had the uncomfortable notion that Chance Cody was not pleased by what he saw.

In fact, the diamond sparks in the coal-black eyes deepened, and the Indian part of him seemed suddenly to be inexplicably intensified.

'God in heaven!' Chance Cody swore in an incredulous, savage voice. 'An impostor.'

CHAPTER TWO

AURORA stood stock still, her very breath frozen. How could he know that? She certainly had no defence planned in the event she was exposed as an impostor within ten minutes of arriving! She had been warned Chance Cody wouldn't like surprises, but she had to admit she hadn't been very concerned about what Chance Cody might, or might not, like. She had certainly not been prepared for a wrath so quietly dangerous that she could feel herself begin to tremble under the dark contemptuous question in his eyes.

Aurora became uncomfortably aware that it was not only Chance watching her silently and expectantly. She was the centre of attention, and, for the first time in her life, she wasn't enjoying that position. She could feel the heat rising in her cheeks as she bore the brunt of the entire group's amazed scrutiny.

'A lady is always composed,' she reminded herself desperately, mentally quoting Madame Lasard of her Swiss finishing school, 'even in the most awkward of situations.' Calling on a memory of that stiff-spined, elegant and refined woman, Aurora quelled the blush and the quivering, and forced her face into an unconcerned and cool mask. She ordered herself to continue to meet his scathing look, unconsciously lifting her chin to hide the fact that for the first time in her life she felt well and truly intimidated.

The midnight eyes left her face, and the breath went out of her in a long sigh of relief. Chance scanned the sky, as if his very will could call back the departed helicopter, and ridiculously Aurora almost believed it would reappear over the trees. It didn't, and her reprieve was short.

'Who are you?' he demanded, his voice made more threatening by the fact that it was terribly quiet and controlled.

Aurora debated. Should she insist she was Mindy? Insist he had made a mistake? It would be delicious if this arrogant tyrant was forced to admit an error . . . forced to apologise to her in front of the group.

'Well?'

Aurora realised she had been fantasising—unrealistically. Chance Cody's eyes were sharp and watchful on her face. It would, she realised with a sigh, take a more practised liar than herself to put one past him. In the light of her inexperience, the lie would be quickly uncovered anyway. Added to that, she had the uneasy sensation that he half expected her to lie, and she proudly refused to give him the satisfaction of being right.

'I'm Aurora Fairhurst,' she said with haughty lack of apology, her green eyes holding his. She was accustomed to seeing recognition, and then, inevitably, deference, creeping into the expressions of those she introduced herself to, but Chance Cody's expression remained hooded and unreadable. If he had recognised the name, he didn't give a damn who she was, but she found it more comforting to assume he lived a rugged and isolated life and had never been exposed to the Fairhurst name—

though it was obvious it was recognised by someone else.

Aurora heard a mutered, 'Well, la-dee-da,' from the dark, outdoorsy young woman. She flicked her a brief, cool look, then returned her gaze to Chance.

'I'm taking Melinda Harrison's place.' She silently thanked Madame Lasard for the calm, almost authoritative note she had managed to pull off.

Black eyes narrowed dangerously and then Chance suddenly seemed to take notice of the group milling about, curious and somewhat anxious about this unexpected development. He turned abruptly from Aurora.

'Danny,' he addressed the sullen-looking youth, 'handle the orientation, and look after the food. Do you remember how I told you I wanted it done?'

'Yessir,' Danny muttered unenthusiastically.

'And you,' Chance turned back to Aurora, and she felt anew the impact of that smouldering glance, 'pick up your pack and come with me.'

Aurora's green eyes threw indignant sparks. How dare he order her about as if she were a—a lackey! A refusal rose on her lips, and then died when his forbidding eyes narrowed with silent warning on her rebellious face.

Flustered, she wordlessly extricated her bright red pack from the cluster of packs, and was unable to suppress a small groan as she hoisted it up, and struggled into the straps. Chance Cody made no offer to help her, sinewy arms folded across his powerful chest, his face impassive. Unsympathetically, he gestured for her to precede him across the clearing, and she did so, aware that he was gauging her every step.

'That trail there,' he ordered from behind her, and she stepped on to the trail, very shortly finding herself on a wide creek bank—and completely isolated from the group. She turned slowly, and regarded Chance apprehensively. One look at his face, and the panic she was struggling to contain threatened to erupt. There was no denying the fury in Chance's eyes, even if his face was icily impassive, and Aurora was unable to suppress a shiver of pure fear at being totally alone with this rugged stranger. She had never in her life felt so totally vulnerable, and her imagination began to run away with her. Surely he wouldn't hit her? Or worse——

Chance did not miss her apprehensive shiver, and his impatience showed in the flicking muscle in his jaw. 'It's been several generations since anyone in my family claimed a scalp,' he said sarcastically. 'You can take off your pack.'

The statement dispelled her fear that she might be in any physical danger and, feeling safer on that count, she allowed herself anger. How dare he use that tone of voice on her? It was curt, and reeked of the confidence of a man who expected unquestionably to be obeyed. Seething, she slipped the straps off her shoulders, and carelessly dropped the pack to the ground. She folded her arms over her chest and watched as Chance removed his own pack.

'So, you are part Indian,' she commented, making it less than a compliment.

He leaned over and picked up her pack with unforgivable ease. 'My great-grandfather was a pure-blooded Stoney.' He let the weight of her pack rest suspended in one hand for a moment, and then set it down, with far more care than she had used.

'I want to know what you're doing here,' he said softly, the subject of his heritage irrevocably closed.

She forced herself to stare staunchly into those dark, cold eyes. 'I already told you,' she proclaimed airily. 'I'm taking Melinda Harrison's place.'

'Perhaps you could tell me a little more.' His mock politeness did not disguise something faintly menacing in his tone. 'What happened to Miss Harrison?'

'I knocked her over the head, stole her ticket, tied her up and stowed her in my closet—but please don't worry about her. The butler should have discovered her by now.'

Reluctant amusement leapt in his eyes but was swiftly veiled. 'I find it very difficult to believe you would find two weeks in the wilderness that irresistible. Which brings me back to my original question—why did you decide to inflict yourself on my expedition?'

Aurora winced at his choice of words. For that brief moment, when a hint of laughter had lit his eyes, she had glimpsed a man capable of dangerous charm. But it didn't take much effort to imagine the women who had succumbed, and she was damned if she'd be one of them! She shrugged stubbornly.

'Does it really matter why I'm here? The fact is, I am here, and, unless you can figure out how to get that helicopter back, you're stuck with that fact.'

His eyes raked her silently. 'I'm well aware of exactly what I'm stuck with, Miss Fairhurst. What I'd like to determine is exactly how being stuck with it is going to affect my expedition.'

'Not in the least,' she assured him haughtily. 'I intend

to just mind my own business and enjoy the scenery.'

'That just told me you're totally ignorant of the types of things that happen on a trip like this. There isn't room for excess baggage.' He paused, and some of the acid faded from his tone. 'Have you ever been on any kind of expedition?'

Excess baggage? 'No,' she managed through clenched teeth.

'A day trip?' he said with hopefulness that didn't sound very hopeful.

She shook her head.

Chance Cody cursed under his breath. 'I'll take legal action against Melinda Harrison if I feel I have to refund the trip expenses to the other hikers because of your presence.'

Aurora digested that, and decided one small admission might not hurt. 'Melinda doesn't know I'm here. You'd be taking on me. And believe me, Mr Cody, you're not big enough to take on Fairhurst.'

A tight, humourless smile met her threat. 'In some circles,' he said softly, 'the Fairhurst Corporation is considered a pretty small fish.'

Aurora stared at him in astonishment. In what circles?

'Let's hope it doesn't come down to a fight, Miss Fairhurst, because you won't win.' In court or anywhere else, by his tone.

She desperately wanted to call his bluff. That had to be a bluff. The Fairhurst Corporation a small fish? Still, Chance Cody did not have the look of a bluffer.

He gestured at the pack. 'Empty it,' he commanded crisply.

Aurora's head snapped up rebelliously. Now was the time to make it clear, in no uncertain terms, that she would not tolerate being bossed around! Chance Cody's arrogant bearing and intimidating manner did not change the fact he was still the hired help, for all his ridiculous insinuations otherwise. As such, he was showing an intolerable lack of respect. After all, her trip was paid for; her money helped pay his wages just like anybody else's!

'Mr Cody,' she breathed coolly, fighting not to back down from the piercing light in those black eyes, and striving for a confidence she didn't feel, 'I don't care for your tone of voice. It's more than obvious you have taken a dislike to me, and I feel compelled to remind you that you rely on people like me for your livelihood.'

Chance Cody looked momentarily stunned, and Aurora felt brief satisfaction. Obviously this barbaric, egotistical mountain man had little experience with being shown his place. But his astonished expression vanished almost immediately, and Aurora had a quick change of heart, wishing she could snatch the words back. His eyes glittered with wicked challenge, like a large cat toying with a mouse, and a heavy brow arched mockingly upward. He watched her thoughtfully, letting her squirm uncomfortably before he spoke.

When he did his voice was low. 'You're quite right on one count, princess,' he said, placing scathing emphasis on the 'princess'. 'I don't think I do like you much. I have a very low tolerance for spoiled brats.' He smiled faintly and without warmth when she sputtered an indignant denial.

'But on the other count, you are quite wrong: I rely on

people like you for absolutely nothing.' His voice was very quiet and ice edged. 'But since you brought the subject up, maybe we'd better talk about reliance. It seems to me, at the moment, you rely totally on me. By your own admission you've never backpacked in your life, and you probably know zip about the land we're about to walk into. You're dead without me,' he stated coldly, not threatening her, but simply stating a fact. 'And you can't get much more dependent than that. Your comfort, your enjoyment, your safety, and your survival rest entirely in my hands. I won't let my personal feelings affect the responsibility I have for you, but I don't expect to have to fight you in order to carry out that responsibility. Is that clear?'

Aurora stared at him, completely unseated by the swift ease with which he had turned the tables and gained the upper hand. He had effectively put her in her place, and the experience was a brand new one, not to mention unpleasant.

She scowled at him petulantly, not at all eager to give him the victory for round one, though she had to concede it was pretty hard to argue with fact. Her life *was* in this man's hands for the next two weeks; she *was* completely at his mercy. But admit it? Say so in as many words? Never!

'I asked if that was clear,' he reminded her, a band of steel running through the soft question. The contest of wills was humiliatingly short.

'Perfectly clear,' she mumbled with ill grace, her eyes stormy.

'Good,' he said softly. 'Now empty your pack, please.' The 'please' was a formality that did nothing to take the autocratic sting out of his command. And it wasn't until she had begun to comply—without an explanation—that he offered one.

'You're going to find the going fairly tough,' he told her flatly, 'without handicapping yourself. Your pack was improperly balanced, and far too heavy. A first time backpacker should never attempt to carry more than a fifth of their body weight.' His gaze moved lazily up and down her length, the blazing intimacy of his eyes causing her to blush for all that the rest of his facial features remained bland and impersonal. 'Which, for you, I'd judge to mean not more than twenty-two pounds. You've got double that in there now, and we haven't even distributed the food yet.'

His guess of her weight was impossibly accurate, and she couldn't deny she had found his eyes moving over her body highly disturbing. The impact of his gaze had been like a physical touch, and she felt seared to her soul.

'I can't get rid of half my things,' she proclaimed, hiding her discomfort in a chilling tone. 'I need everything I brought.'

'That's highly doubtful,' he informed her drily, flicking a practised eye over the items she had removed from her pack. 'Start separating that into two piles. In one I want only the things you absolutely need for survival, in the other you can put everything else.'

Ungraciously, Aurora moved a few items into a separate stack, but even those she gazed at wistfully. The battery-operated hairdryer was so small and practical, and weighed next to nothing.

'Survival, Aurora,' Chance repeated with soft insistence, 'not the débutante ball.'

Sarcastic boor, she thought glaring at him. Sullenly she debated over a few more items, and moved them. 'That's it,' she announced imperiously.

Chance sighed impatiently, and squatted on his heels beside her, one massive shoulder brushing hers. Aurora could feel herself tensing at his touch, and felt stunned by the sudden trembling of her heart. She had to acknowledge that she was acutely and uncomfortably aware of Chance Cody as a man. Acutely aware of the muscle beneath his shirt, and of the clean, masculine scent of him. Acutely aware, suddenly and unexpectedly, of herself as a woman, and of the differences between man and woman. Aware of how her curves and her softness were made somehow to melt into his straight, lean lines, and his hardness. Aware that she had never felt such a compelling force before ... not with Sven, and certainly not with Douglas.

For the second time in a single day she found herself questioning her sanity. She absolutely abhorred this man beside her. Why, then, did such a casual touch cause her senses to riot? Perhaps, she tried to console herself, the very strength of her antipathy had something to do with it, had set her nerves on end. Perhaps her physical reaction was just mirroring her prickling, jarred emotions.

Chance, apparently oblivious to the havoc he was wreaking on her senses, and without consulting her, began to shift other items into her 'unessential' pile. He completely ignored her gasps of indignation and dismay, though Aurora had to admit they were rather weak; her fight was being concentrated on trying to ignore the electrical sensations caused by his shoulder still brushing hers.

'Cosmetics are not essential,' Chance said, the deep voice breaking into her whirling, wayward thoughts.

'They are for me!' Aurora protested, managing to struggle back to the surface of reality. The very idea of appearing without make-up genuinely horrified her. Madame Lasard had been brutally frank in her assessment of Aurora's facial features—'Nice, but very plain; nothing spectacular, except maybe your eyes. Not to worry, though, any woman can achieve the illusion of being spectacular with clever and skilled use of cosmetics.' Aurora realised with abrupt dismay that a great deal of her confidence depended on that clever and skilled use of make-up. It made the difference between being plain and being attractive, and she desperately wanted Chance Cody to find her fascinatingly attractive—mostly so that she could have the pleasure of not returning his attentions!

Chance took in her panicked expression without sympathy, and caught her hand in an iron grip when she reached once more for her cosmetics kit. 'No,' he said firmly. 'The weight is unnecessary, and you won't have time to be fooling around with it anyway.' He released her hand but the electricity of his touch continued to shiver up her arm, making her disagreeably aware—again—of his manhood. The traitorous reaction of her body made her begin to hate him passionately, but she made no attempt to risk the brush of his hand again to rescue her cosmetics.

He had already moved on, unmoved by her pout. He picked up the thick, sizzling romantic novel she had brought along, and smiled sardonically, then turned mocking, slightly wicked black eyes back to her.

'Your fiancé not providing enough real-life passion for you, Aurora?' he queried softly, his tone suggesting the women in his life had all the passion they could handle without having to look for any more between the pages of books.

Aurora glared at him. How had he guessed she was engaged? Then she remembered the large diamond-studded engagement ring that she wore on her left hand. She decided it shouldn't surprise her that nothing escaped those eyes that glittered with something approaching animal alertness.

The idea of Douglas being passionate should have been laughable. Instead the question stung her oddly. It filled her with doubts about her own ability to inspire passion, and it caused a strange longing within her to know a mystery that had eluded her. She looked quickly away from those sharp, too-observant eyes, purposely letting her hair fall to curtain her profile from him.

'Douglas is a gentleman!' she exclaimed, her voice a little too shrill in her own ears.

'How very dull for you,' Chance taunted mildly. He tossed the book away. 'I'm not,' he stated flatly.

'That,' Aurora spluttered, 'is more than evident!'

Chance responded by reaching over and pushing away the veil of hair she had let slip down to guard her face from his gaze.

'What does your husband-to-be think of your sudden interest in Canada's great north?' The question was asked with seeming casualness, but the dark eyes were probing.

Aurora hardly realised she flinched at the reference to Douglas as her 'husband-to-be'.

'In case it slipped your notice,' she said coolly, 'women have had independence for some time. I hardly consider it necessary to discuss all my plans with Douglas.'

The eyes were watchful, uncomfortably astute. 'If you were my intended, you wouldn't be spending two weeks running around in the bush without my knowledge—in fact, considering your lack of experience, you wouldn't be spending two weeks in the bush at all.'

'Oh?' She raised an eyebrow. 'And how do you think you would have stopped me?'

'By keeping you satisfied at home.' The silky sensuality of his voice made his implication clear and Aurora gasped.

'Savage!' she sputtered.

His expression was dark and enigmatic. 'The thin veneers of civilisation don't last very long in the wilderness,' he said with soft arrogance. 'The senses become very sharply honed. Instinct that we've almost forgotten was born into us rises closer to the surface. We become more aware of our natural drives, and more at home with them.'

He paused, enjoying her shocked expression, and then continued softly. 'Your eyes spit green sparks, Aurora Fairhurst. Has your fiancé attempted to tame the tigress lurking behind that polished mask? Does he appreciate your fire and your passion and your hunger, as I would? As I might?' He was smiling at her with wolfish menace.

'Mr Cody!' Aurora reprimanded him stiffly. 'If there is a passionate side to my nature, I assure you *you* will never see it! In our short acquaintance I have decided I despise you as much as any single person I have ever met!'

'If?' he taunted, his eyebrows shooting up. 'And don't worry, our baser yearnings usually don't let a little thing like whether we like a person get in the way of what they want.'

'You are talking about lust,' Aurora stated with pure disgust, though her heart was thudding crazily against her chest, and her stomach had the queerest feeling in it. This very discussion seemed to be encouraging a wilder side of her closer to the surface. The man beside her exuded a rugged virility that seemed to make even the burning resentment she felt for him a petty and inconsequential thing.

'Lust,' Chance agreed unapologetically. 'Pity you've been ingrained with a learned revulsion for the word. I don't understand that attitude, personally. There's something awesomely beautiful about life's longing to recreate itself—about an instinct so powerful and so insistent that the human race manages to survive despite everything. Despite taboos and Puritan eras, and the attempts to instil a sense of shame and embarrassment in young people concerning their bodies and their sensuality, it survives. All that carefully nurtured restraint and reserve are swept away, forgotten, when a certain man meets a certain woman, and they acknowledge the primal hunger that exists in them. I think it's magnificent. Don't you?'

'I do not!' Aurora exclaimed primly, her primness increased by her horror at the renegade question her mind asked her. *What would it feel like if those firm lips were to capture yours?* it prompted shamelessly.

Having thoroughly riled her, Chance abandoned the subject as carelessly as he had entered into it, apparently unaware of the tension he had created. He continued rummaging through her things, leaving Aurora to glare accusingly and ineffectually at him. What kind of man openly discussed a subject like lust with a woman he barely knew? A savage, she answered herself; an uncouth, overbearing, odious monster—who happened to have a body she was suddenly achingly aware of. She ground her teeth together. No doubt he was quite accustomed to women panting over his broad-shouldered brawn—to the point where he didn't even try to polish his rough personality!

He had known, she concluded suspiciously, he had known when he started this conversation that it would make her aware of the immense virility he exuded, make her aware of his dangerous and enticing masculinity. Well, if Chance Cody thought for one minute that she would lose control of herself—give into that primal hunger—he was dead wrong! She would show him . . . wouldn't she?

'What in God's name——'

Aurora's breath caught in her throat, and she almost expected Chance had read her mind. She peered warily at him, relieved to see that he wasn't watching her at all, but looking with impatient bafflement at a large box of mothballs.

Aurora was quicker than him this time, and she snatched the box from his hands. 'I have to have these.'

'What the hell are they for?' Chance bit out impatiently.

'To scare bears,' she told him firmly, hugging the

large box close to herself.

'To scare bears,' Chance repeated incredulously, a quirk at the corner of his mouth threatening his stern demeanour.

Weakly, Aurora explained Davie's reassurance to him.

'I don't suppose it occurred to you that the smell of mothballs isn't going to be particularly enchanting to anyone?' The humour she had suspected a moment ago had already vanished, and a thin line of exasperation ran through his tone.

'So?' she demanded, clutching her mothballs even tighter.

'So, nobody is here, princess, to have their senses assaulted with the stink of mothballs lingering in the air. I think pine, and wood smoke, and the scent of the sun warming the earth are more what the expectations run to.'

'I don't care,' Aurora said stubbornly.

The grim expression on his face deepened. 'No, I didn't figure you for much of a team player. No one else'e enjoyment concerns you in the least, does it? If it did, you wouldn't be here in the first place.'

'I don't think my presence has the slightest chance of threatening anyone's enjoyment,' she proclaimed stiffly.

He looked pointedly at the mothballs, and let his eyes drift back to her face, but said nothing.

Angrily, she thrust the box at him. 'I want you to know I'm holding you personally responsible if I get eaten by a bear.'

'Fine,' he agreed drily, tossing the mothballs carelessly on top of her other possessions that would be left behind.

'I hope you have a gun?'

'I don't ever carry a rifle when I'm packing,' he told her sharply, and then sighed when she paled before his eyes. 'If it makes you feel any better, I've been leading trips like this one for a long time. I have yet to lose anyone to a bear.'

Aurora did not look—or feel—reassured, and Chance sighed. 'Look, Aurora, bears are wild animals, and yes, they can be dangerous. But usually a wild animal, particularly one who has been isolated from man, will be far more frightened of you than you are of him. We'll take every precaution, and as soon as possible, I'll brief you on what to do in the unlikely event of an encounter with a bruin.'

He picked up her tiny bottle of Shalimar. 'Meanwhile, we'll leave this here. Most experienced hikers know that perfumes and cosmetics sometimes contain an animal musk that is irresistible to bears.'

Aurora gave a muffled shriek, picked up her flannel, and headed for the creek. She unhesitatingly washed off her perfume and every scrap of make-up.

'That's how you knew that I—er—had taken someone's place,' she guessed when she returned.

'That's one of the ways I knew,' Chance agreed, 'but there were also the brand new clothes and boots, your long fingernails, the general lack of muscle tone . . .' He shrugged, and returned his attention to her things, leaving her glaring at him. Lack of muscle tone? she screeched inwardly. Why, the insulting cad——

'A flashlight?' He interrupted her thoughts.

She sensed his irritation. 'I would have thought that

was fairly standard on a camping trip,' she defended herself huffily.

'You're in the land of the midnight sun,' Chance bit out coldly. 'At this time of year, we'll be getting about twenty-two hours of light daily.'

'Then I guess I won't need the flashlight,' Aurora snapped unapologetically, refusing to shrink from the blackness in those devastating eyes.

He returned to her belongings, and picked up her large, thick bath towel. 'Think half of this would do?' he asked, his knife already poised at the edge.

'I think you're being a little bit fanatical,' she muttered. 'How much does half a towel weigh?'

He ignored her, cut the edging, replaced his knife in its hilt, and then ripped the towel in two as easily as if it were a sheet of paper. Aurora saw his eye flick across the label with casual interest. The interest struck her as odd and out of character, and she picked up the towel when he had cast it aside.

Richly embroidered and elegant script spelled out a single word. A legend, really. Robards.

She looked up at Chance, and knew immediately he was annoyed, either at her for picking up on his interest, or at himself for letting it show.

'Do you have some connection with Robards?'

'Maybe.' The unrevealing statement was made coldly, and he didn't elaborate. Aurora eyed him narrowly. Robards certainly was big—yes, big enough to call Fairhurst a small fish. But what could this earthy, self-assured wilderness guide have to do with an international company of that size and reputation? Did Madame Robards own the guide outfit? She certainly might—without even being aware of the fact.

Chance had not missed a beat and he stripped her of her camera, and her tent, insisting it was too heavy and she would have to share accommodation with the other young woman, Heather. With swift efficiency he took her boots and wet them to make the leather more pliable on her tender feet, applied some tincture of benizon to her toes, repacked her belongings, and proclaimed her as ready as she'd ever be for the trail.

They returned to the main group just as Danny was folding up the maps. Aurora's pack, though she refused to say a grateful word to Chance, felt wonderfully light.

Chance immediately reassumed his role as leader, suggesting the group do a quick introduction session before heading off. Aurora got the distinct impression he didn't particularly like this part of the first day, and would have just as readily headed off without the group introducing themselves.

Modesty? she thought with surprise. Huh! Chance Cody probably just disliked sharing any details about himself with mere mortals.

Scott Rawley, one of the twins, started it of. At twenty-six he was older than he looked, and Aurora was surprised he'd been practising dentistry for a year.

'I've been fishing and camping and hiking with my Dad and my brother since before I can remember. I've been dreaming of this trip for nearly five years—it's the big reward I promised myself on those twenty-cups-of-coffee-nights when it seemed it would be easier to give up than finish school.'

The other twin drew a laugh when he repeated his

brother's biography exactly, adding only that his name was Hank.

'Miss la-dee-da' was Heather Carter, a physical education teacher from the mid-western United States. As well as listing mountaineering experiences that made Aurora's head spin, she was a championship-level clay pigeon shooter, and her hobbies included running and aerobics. Aurora noticed grumpily that *she* certainly didn't lack muscle tone.

It was Aurora's turn, and she stifled the feeling of inadequacy she felt, unapologetically reciting only her name, age and where she was from.

'Danny, your turn,' Chance prompted.

The youth looked at Chance with hostility, and then looked at his hands. 'My name's Danny Jones.' He shot Chance another look, and Aurora could have sworn she saw faint pleading in it. She glanced at Chance. If he had noticed the pleading, he was unmoved by it. 'And if I wasn't here, I'd be in jail,' the boy finished in nearly a whisper.

Aurora glared at Chance. An inhuman, insensitive beast, just as she'd suspected, she thought with faint satisfaction.

Chance spoke last, outlining briefly his experience as an instructor, leader and guide with various outdoor ventures and wilderness and mountaineering programmes. Aurora found his biography left more questions than it answered. There was far more to Chance Cody than his brief sketch allowed, and she was ridiculously eager to hear all of it.

Her curiosity about the man did not please her at all, and she feared he might sense it, and come to the conclusion she was interested in him. Annoyed with herself for being so interested, and in him for not assuaging her curiosity, she turned to him with a haughty look.

'Nice little group,' she said caustically. 'Let's see, we have the Bobbsey Twins, Annie Oakley, an ex-convict, and the reincarnation of Daniel Boone.'

Chance looked at her with cold dislike, and she had the satisfied feeling he would have dearly liked to smack her. Knowing she had effectively covered up the fact that the sum of the group's experience made her feel self-conscious, intimidated and even a little guilty about being here, eased her feelings of inadequacy slightly.

Chance Cody met her gaze evenly and a tight smile curled cruelly over his firm mouth. 'You forgot someone,' he told her with biting curtness. 'You forgot the one that nobody else is going to be able to forget—Princess Aurora.' Abruptly he turned on his heel, and strode away.

Aurora squinted narrowly after him. Surely his teaming of the 'princess' with her name was coincidental and not clever? He was too far from boyhood to recall fairytales, and it was ludicrous to think Chance Cody might share her mother's enthusiasm for the ballet.

If her mother had done one unpredictable thing in her life, it was probably to call her daughter Aurora. Her father had wanted her named after a very old—and very rich—maiden aunt. But Edna, uncharacteristically, had stood up to her husband, and Aurora sometimes wondered if some spark of romance, long since gone, had once beat within her rigid-faced mother's breast.

In the naming of Aurora had she passed on to her

daughter her wistful longing for romantic fulfilment? Had there been a vague, subconscious hope that her daughter would find a prince, rather than being channelled into a marriage of convenience, as she had been?

Aurora pulled herself up short. It was highly unlikely that her mother had been motivated by anything but a deep admiration of the ballet. Besides which, Aurora suddenly found it extremely uncomfortable to be thinking about a sleeping princess waiting for a kiss to awaken her ...

CHAPTER THREE

AURORA could sense excited anticipation from the others as the group prepared to start off into the woods. She didn't share the feeling, hiding her apprehension behind a bored, cool mask. She glanced around the clearing with inner wistfulness, admitting an odd attachment to it. It seemed safe and sunshiny, wide open and resplendent in wild flowers. On the other hand, the woods all around looked dark and brooding, frightening and full of secrets ... not to mention, quite probably, bears. The clearing had eased some of her initial fear of this endless and overwhelming wilderness, but now she was once again heading into the unknown and she didn't like it one bit.

She watched with studied indifference as Chance assigned everyone to places in the line. Finally he came to her, and, just to underscore the fact that she wasn't impressed—or the least bit afraid—she yawned daintily behind her hand.

His face was remote, his eyes flinty, as he looked at her. When he spoke his voice held a quality of cold professionalism.

'You'll follow Heather. Keep about ten feet between you. Danny's the end-man and he'll follow you.'

His glance flicked down her, assessing and impersonal. His eyes stopped on the straps of her backpack, and he reached out and placed strong fingers underneath the padded bands, testing the tension—and creating an unwanted tension in her as his hands followed the line of the straps from her shoulders downward, his knuckles, by necessity, brushing the outer curves of her breasts.

He leaned forward, engrossed in some adjustment he was making to her strap, and Aurora, indifference forgotten, wondered desperately if he could feel the trembling of her heart, sense the heat that was rising in her to answer the heat created by the brief, casual brushes of those lean, brown hands. He finally stepped back, and took in her blush with a wickedly raised eyebrow.

'How does that feel?' he asked, his voice entirely and insufferably composed.

'What?' she stammered stupidly, her blush deepening at the devilish amusement that leapt sparkling into the pools of black. Not even all Madame Lasard's rigid preparation could keep her composed in an awkward situation of this magnitude! Damn him! Didn't he feel anything at all? Didn't he feel slightly shaky? Couldn't he feel the sparks hissing dangerously in the air between them? Wasn't he in the least attracted to her as a woman—personality differences aside?

'The straps.' He answered her question drily and evenly, his tone assuring her he didn't feel in the slightest bit shaky.

'Fine,' she answered, hating him. He had known what he was doing! How dared he mock her? Play with her? Use his damned virility to knock down her defences when she needed her defences most?

He turned abruptly away from her. 'Let's move out,'

he called, making his way with that long, loose-limbed stride up to his place at the front of the line.

They began to move, but Aurora's fear of the dark, forbidding forest had been edged out by a greater fear—of a man with dark, forbidding eyes. Why was she reacting this way to him? It baffled and enraged her. Even Sven, with whom she had exchanged a few exploratory kisses, had never aroused in her this slightly out-of-control feeling that she could only define as passion. Sven, she thought bitterly, who had used her. Chance would be no different. He would use her, too, but in a far more frightening and damaging way than Sven ever had. Chance had made it clear exactly how he would use her if she was ever fool enough to give in to the overwhelming and entirely senseless emotions that he seemed capable of arousing in her.

She thought of the malicious remarks she had made about the group, and sudden self-understanding took her aback. It wasn't just her own inadequacy they were meant to mask. No, they had been designed by a frightened subconscious to make sure Chance despised her, kept his distance, thereby protecting her from her traitorous self and from being used again. But she was treading a fine line. To make Chance too angry might be to bring his wrath down upon her in exactly the way she most feared. Or had her rotten subconscious already figured out that angle? Figured out that the frightened child was almost ready, almost ripe to discover the secret wells of passion inside herself that she had denied for too long. Was she subconsciously letting go of past hurts, acknowledging the slow healing of the past year, listening to a bolder part that insisted on coming forward?

Chance had talked about nature, and it occurred to Aurora now that nature played a big part in the fact that twenty-two year old virgins were rather a rarity. She had been denying a part of herself, repressing it stubbornly and fearfully. But the gaze of Chance's dark and mysterious eyes seemed to call it out of her—tease her and taunt her, as if those eyes knew more about her than she knew about herself. The door to the secret place within her was open a crack, she realised, and now she could feel powerful forces pushing against it insistently, threatening to blow the very hinges off the door.

No! she told herself fiercely. I won't give in! I won't give in to the niggling curiosity, or that funny ache that seems to yearn for something I've never known. I won't! And especially not with Chance Cody I won't! Had she completely flipped her lid? The man had behaved outrageously! He had humiliated her, put her in her place, and been insufferably rude about doing it.

She retreated swiftly from her tumultuous thoughts into a world more familiar to her. With super-human effort she slammed shut that door within her, and called forth instead memories of a world—her world—where everything, even the courting rituals, was refined and well-ordered and polished. Maybe it was because he had made a reference to a débutante ball earlier that she thought of that. Thought of herself in her swirling white dress, with her hair piled high, thought of her low, sweeping curtsy, and the young men, impeccably dressed in tails and velvet bow ties, who had bent low over her gloved hand. It was a world as far removed from Chance Cody as she could get, and she tried to remember it in exacting romantic detail. She tried to tell herself that that was the correct and proper way for men and women to meet and fall in love. Primal hunger, indeed!

Yet she was having trouble convincing herself—having a great deal of trouble overcoming a niggling small voice that asked her if the *real* Aurora Fairhurst had enjoyed all the pomp and circumstance, or if some unacknowledged part of herself hadn't found it boring, superficial and phoney.

Of course it hadn't been phoney, Aurora informed herself doubtfully, and then sighed. The unknown was not just outside her now, but inside, too.

The first break was called, and Aurora felt proud of herself. Nothing to it, she silently and smugly informed Chance's back. She had known there was not the least chance of her threatening his precious group's enjoyment.

Still, she was quite eager to divest herself of the pack and have a cup of tea. But when she started to remove it, Chance materialised beside her, stopping her, easing it back up into place. Deft fingers unbuckled the belt at her waist.

'We'll only be stopped for two or three minutes,' he told her. 'Lean over from the waist and lock your hands on your knees.'

'You must be joking!' she snapped incredulously, her smugness forgotten as she tilted her head back to look up at him. 'A three-minute break? We've been walking for hours.'

'One hour,' he informed her drily. 'A longer break would just give your muscles time to stiffen up, and make it harder to get started again.'

'But I want a cup of tea!' she almost wailed.

'Have a drink of water,' he suggested unsympathetically. 'How are your feet?'

'Still there,' she snapped.

'If you feel a hotspot coming up, let me know immediately.' His voice had that overbearing, autocratic note in it that Aurora despised. It held not the least pretence of concern. Chance Cody was just doing his job, nothing more and nothing less!

'Certainly,' she agreed sweetly, deciding then and there that her legs would have to fall of before she asked him for assistance!

Somehow Aurora managed to force herself to keep walking until lunchtime, and proudly refrained from telling anyone, least of all Chance Cody, about the irritating, painful burning in several places on her feet.

Shortly after she had sat down and was miserably spreading peanut butter on a hard cracker while dreaming of a grilled steak and baked potato, Chance appeared before her, towering over her, barely contained anger written in every line of that rugged face.

'I thought I told you to tell me if you were having trouble with your feet,' he snapped.

'My feet are fine,' she lied, biting into her unappetising cracker with pretended unconcern.

'Oh? Do you limp as a matter of course?' he asked roughly.

'How do you know if I'm limping?' she challenged. Chance had been moving back and forth along the line all morning, and she had noticed he was monitoring her closely. Some sixth sense always told her when his eyes were resting on her, and she managed to hide the growing limp—even managed to smile carelessly and put a little spring in her step when those black eyes narrowed gaugingly on her.

'Danny noticed and told me.'

'Little snitch,' she muttered mutinously.

'He was doing his job,' Chance informed her tersely. 'I asked him to keep an eye on you—though I didn't think you'd be fool enough to let mulish pride threaten your own well-being.'

'I hardly think a blister could be considered a threat to my well-being,' she retorted, her tone accusing him of overreacting—looking for any excuse to berate her unjustly.

His eyes narrowed and his voice became very soft. 'Survival in the wilderness is quite often a case of stopping problems before they start. I was once on an expedition where we had to evacuate a member because of blisters. And if you think an evacuation in this country is fun, you had better think again.'

'Oh,' she said, but not very contritely. The idea of being carried out of here on a stretcher was infintely appealing at the moment.

'Finish your lunch,' he ordered curtly, 'and then I'll look after your feet.'

'Since you mention lunch,' she said, determined to get in the last word over this brow-beating brute, 'I'd like to register a complaint. Really, for the expense of the trip, I expected a little more substantial fare than peanut butter and crackers.'

'Did you now, princess?' he queried softly, and though his tone was controlled and almost bored, a muscle in his jaw was fascinating her by tensing and untensing in rapid jerks. 'You'll have to forgive me—I forgot to pack the chef.' He paused. 'Don't push me too far, Aurora,' he warned in a low voice that set her heart to hammering. The fiery pride of his ancestors was burning in his eyes, and she could see the faint cruel twist of his mouth.

'Push you?' she said innocently. 'I just thought I'd mention it.' But for some reason, when he turned and walked away the air came out of her with a heartfelt hiss of relief.

A short while later, Aurora found herself seated on a fallen log while Chance knelt on the ground in front of her, his hands moving over her feet. She stared down at the top of his black head, mesmerised by his unbelievable gentleness as he ministered to her feet. Who would have thought this tyrant's powerful, lean hands would have been capable of such a featherlight touch?

'That hurt there?' He glanced briefly up at her face, his own wearing that infernal expression of impassive professionalism that she was coming to profoundly hate.

It was as if the hands and face belonged to two separate people—one arousing in her a strange yearning, the other a dislike as powerful as anything she had ever felt! She nodded curtly in answer to his question.

He cut off yet another piece of moleskin to put over the delicate area. 'I think that's it. I'm just going to drain those two blisters, and you'll be all ready for an afternoon of fun in the wilderness.'

'I think it would have been more fun to join the Marines,' she returned waspishly, her eyes widening as he reached into the canvas medical bag beside him and unwrapped a needle from its sterilised package.

'You're not sticking that thing in my foot,' she howled, and jerked away from him. She lost her balance and fell over the back of the log with an ungraceful plonk, her legs still resting against it, and sticking straight up in the air. Before she could alter her undignified position, Chance was on his feet, and had snared her ankle.

'Quit squirming,' he ordered. 'It won't hurt.' He grinned down at her with devilish amusement, obviously finding her helpless position most satisfying. Aurora huffed indignantly, quashing the part of her that oohed like a schoolgirl over the flash of strong, brilliantly white teeth contrasting with his bronzed skin. This man was an insufferable rogue. She refused to see him as attractive and she must have imagined the near tenderness of his touch a moment ago!

'I told you to hold still,' he warned. 'I'm holding a small but sharp object in my hand.'

She stiffened, folded her arms over her chest, and stared mutinously up at the sky, preparing to scream the whole forest down as soon as he stuck that needle in her foot. Let the whole camp know that he was a fiend! That he enjoyed inflicting pain——

'All done.'

'What do you mean, all done?' she asked disbelievingly, taking her eyes from the sky, and trying to mask the fact she felt cheated of her opportunity to scream.

He reached over and pulled her, none too gently, back on to the log. 'I told you it wouldn't hurt. You needn't look so disappointed. I'm not quite the savage you'd like me to be—and I'm definitely not a member of the "pain is gain" school of thought.' His eyes ridiculed her, making her feel like her thoughts were an open book to him. Please, God, not all of them, she thought desperately.

'I hope that's it for the heroics,' he stated flatly, the 'hope' a definite command. 'I'll expect any further foot problems to be reported immediately.'

'You have a terrible bedside manner,' she spat at him with a spirited toss of her heavy shimmering hair.

A muted light came on in the black, bottomless depths of his eyes, and they swept her, lingering on her hair, and then her lips, and then swinging impertinently lower before moving back to her face. 'I've had no complaints,' he informed her softly, his innuendo unmistakable. Aurora chose to ignore it.

'Well, you have one now!' she told him incautiously.

'Would you like to find out what my bedside manner is *really* like, princess?' he drawled mockingly.

'I told you, I despise you,' she gasped, blushing.

He smiled, a faint, slow smile, and she was reminded of a large cat, watching its prey indolently. 'And I told you that doesn't necessarily have anything to do with it.'

'Mr Cody, don't try to frighten me into docility by making veiled threats of rape,' she returned, her spirit somewhat forced.

'Rape?' A black eyebrow arched upward. 'That's hardly my style.'

'Well, I certainly don't find you appealing enough to allow you to seduce me,' she threw back, and then realised warily she was way out of her depth.

'Should I read that as a challenge?' he taunted, eyes so black, resting on her face, mesmerising her, chasing away her reason, inviting her, drawing her nearer...

She paled. Should he? 'No! This is a ridiculous conversation. I have a fiancé.'

Chance's look was long and searching, laying bare her soul, the spark of his eyes starting a flame within her. He gave her a slow smile—part mysterious, and part predatory—swung abruptly on his heel and walked away.

Aurora's chagrin over Chance's insolent behaviour carried her part of the way through the afternoon. Now that she wasn't actually being subjected to the merciless shimmer of pitch black eyes it was easy to hate him—difficult to imagine what seemed to possess her when she was in his presence. He was arrogant, egotistical, far too sure of his charms, wicked, unreasonable, bad-tempered, judgmental... Her list kept her well occupied, but finally not even that was enough.

Bone-numbing exhaustion had been slowly pushing its way into her awareness and now it took over completely. For a while she was able to keep herself going with pride and a determined little chant of 'one foot after the other', but then irritable temper began to creep in. Why on earth was she torturing herself? She didn't have any reason to try and impress Chance Cody, or anyone else! Why should she keep going, anyway? Why should she push beyond the limits of her endurance? Nobody had the right to ask that of her! Let him sue! It would serve her father right since, indirectly, it was all his fault she was here in the first place.

She was tired, and her feet hurt, and her back hurt, and there was sweat dripping in her eyes and under her armpits. Sweat! She remembered a little line Madame

Lasard used to quote: 'Horses sweat, men perspire, and ladies become dewy.' Have I got news for her, Aurora thought blackly.

Heather, she noted, was well ahead of her on the trail and disappearing around a corner, and not sweating. Aurora was sick of trying to keep up. It was stupid. It was senseless to keep walking around. What was fun about it? It wasn't even adventurous, for pity's sake! It was just painful, and exhausting, and hard work; she wasn't going another step. She stopped abruptly, folded her legs and crumpled into a contented heap in the middle of the trail.

'Hey, lady, what happened? You trip?'

Aurora opened her eyes and glared at Danny. 'No, I did not trip. I quit. Q-U-I-T. Finished. No more. Nap time. I have had enough!'

Danny looked at her, perplexed, and then glanced anxiously at the empty trail in front of him. 'I don't think this is allowed.'

'Toughers,' Aurora said, and closed her eyes. She opened them only long enough to glare at Danny when he let out a long piercing whistle.

'You're weird,' the boy muttered.

There was something vaguely offensive about being called weird by a convicted criminal, but not knowing what kind of behaviour to expect from convicted criminals, even puny ones, Aurora decided to let it pass.

She could hear feet pounding down the path. 'Here comes the cavalry,' she mumbled uncaringly, refusing to open her eyes.

'Weird,' Danny muttered again to himself.

'Is she hurt?'

Aurora recognised the deep voice without much surprise, though the concern in it surprised her a great deal. She felt a momentary pang of guilt—very momentary. Let him worry! He deserved to feel a little anxiety for being so brutally insensitive to her capabilities—or lack of them.

'No, she ain't hurt. She says she quit.'

Aurora heard breath being let out in a long, exasperated hiss, and opened one eye warily. Chance's face looked like thunder. She closed her eye quickly.

'You handled that well, Danny. I'm proud of you. Go ahead and join the others—and tell Scott everything's OK.'

Aurora listened to the boy's footsteps retreating.

'Wake up, princess, or the prince is going to kiss you.'

So, he was clever, Aurora admitted ruefully. She might have even admitted he had a sense of humour, except that the words were not spoken with even a trace of humour, or even mockery—they were spoken with quiet, very dangerous anger, calculated to get her up fast and without argument.

Aurora sat up swiftly and glared at Chance. 'I can't go a step further! I can't!'

'I could have done without the dramatics. Why didn't you just ask for a rest?' he demanded angrily.

'Because I don't want one of those silly three-second wonders you call a rest! I want to stop! I want to stay right here!' Her authentic desperation even surprised her.

Chance sighed, and some of the harshness left his face. 'I know it's hard, Aurora, and I know you're tired. But right now you're just quitting, not because you *can't* make it, but because you don't want to. If I thought you'd given it your best shot, I wouldn't hesitate to stop. An honest try is as good as a goal in this game. But just quitting because it isn't fun, or because it's hard work, or because you don't feel like it, doesn't cut any ice, princess. Not up here, and not in the real world—at least not in the real world as most people know it. I want your best effort. I want you to keep going.'

'Why should I?' she demanded, knowing she sounded childish and stubborn, and not caring one little bit.

'One, it would probably be good for *you*, and two, it would be nice if you at least tried not to spoil this trip for the other people involved.'

'What have they ever done for me?' she snapped churlishly.

His lips tightened, but his tone remained patient. 'Like most sports, this one depends on just the right mix of independence and inter-reliance. This group of people are on their way to becoming a team, Aurora. Like it or not, you're a part of that team. You make some sacrifices for the team—today that means going an extra mile when you don't feel like it—and they make some sacrifices for you. There isn't a person here who couldn't have gone a lot faster and further today. But they didn't, because you're a member of the team, and they're willing to make some concessions for your inexperience—even though they should never have had to on a trip geared to their level of experience.'

'Rah-rah,' she said sourly, but she was getting reluctantly to her feet.

'Good girl,' he said, taking her hand and helping her up. 'We haven't that much further to go for the day.'

'Hurray for small miracles,' she muttered, snatching her hand away from his before she found its strength and solidness so comforting she'd be unable to let go.

Chance looked at her shrewdly. 'Are you practising the breath control techniques that I explained to you?'

Aurora looked at her feet. 'Well—no.' She glanced up at him defiantly. 'I tried, but I got mixed up trying to remember what to do.'

'I'll show you again,' he said patiently. 'I know it seems complicated and unnatural at first, but, if you stick with it, you'll find you won't be nearly so winded at this time of day.'

An hour later they walked into the camp, Chance still beside her, tolerantly coaching her on how to control her breathing.

She looked around her and felt a sensation of triumph pushing its way through the haze of her exhaustion. The feeling stunned her with its strength. It was quite different from anything she had ever felt before; it came from so deep within her. Her feelings of triumph before had always been related to something outside of herself, like having the prettiest dress at a party, or the flashiest car at the country club. This was different—incredibly different, somehow.

Real, a little voice informed her, not without satisfaction.

She became aware of Chance looking down at her with a slightly knowing smile playing across his lips and she scowled at him, surrendering that heady moment of pride in her own strength and forbearance.

Darn him, he had manipulated her! Somehow talked her into doing something she had decided firmly and irrevocably she was not going to do! And now he stood there looking at her, as if he knew somehow that she was grudgingly glad she had done it, as if he understood how satisfied she really felt about her victory over those last few miles of rugged terrain. No doubt he was feeling very smug about his own victory!

She met his gaze impassively. 'Chance Cody, you could make a fortune selling snowballs to Eskimos. You make me sick.' Her head high, she marched away from the blazing amusement in his eyes.

CHAPTER FOUR

'AURORA, give Scott a hand with the latrine.'

Aurora's mouth fell open in shock, and then she crossed her arms with slow deliberateness across her chest, and narrowed her eyes at Chance. It was their third night on the trail, and the first time she had been asked to contribute to the setting-up-camp chores.

'I will not.' She put slow and haughty emphasis on each word.

Chance, cocky in his assurance of his every word being complied with, had already turned away. Now he turned back and gave her a measuring look. 'Why not?' he asked with soft challenge.

Her nose shot into the air. 'Fairhursts do not dig latrines.' A formidable expression appeared on his face, and she hastily tacked on, 'Besides, I'm exhausted.'

'You looked much stronger today.'

'Are you telling me I'm not exhausted?' she demanded.

A twinkle of a smile appeared in his eyes. 'You must be feeling a little better—it's been nearly two whole days since you crossed swords with me.'

It was true, she hadn't even been able to work up enough energy to fight with Chance. Not that there had been any need to. Chance seemed to recognise she was hardly fighting fit, and, though he wasn't exactly kind to her, he was coolly and correctly polite, and often very helpful—though his attitude made it clear any help from him was extended purely in the line of duty.

To soothe her nearly shattered dignity, Aurora had allowed herself to hope her status was being conceded to. Surely a Fairhurst wouldn't be expected to cook meals, wash dishes, or—ye gods!—dig latrines? But in her heart she knew Chance, of all people, would not make any concessions to status. She had hoped he had just decided it would be more trouble than it was worth to include her on the daily work lists.

More realistically, though she hated to admit it because it implied a measure of compassion in the towering, dark-eyed leader, she guessed that Chance knew she was dog-tired, and accepted her efforts on the trail as all she had been capable of—and now he was letting her know the honeymoon was over. More of her inadequacies were going to be put on display for the general amusement of the other hikers.

Not that her fellow travellers had been unfair to her, she had to admit grudgingly. Scott and Hank almost overwhelmed her with their patience, sympathy and good humour. If the trip they had planned for five years was a bit of a disappointment because of her, they had never once let on by word or by action.

Even some of Danny's habitual sullenness seemed to fall away around her. With a start she realised the initial wariness she had felt for Danny—people in her circle did not rub elbows with ex-convicts—had dwindled to nothing. He was just a kid—true, a rather strange and troubled kid, but a kid all the same. Behind that deadpan, hooded expression, Aurora had discovered a sharp, if cynical, sense of humour that quite charmed her, and more than once they shared a quick snicker at something one of them had to say about Chance. She supposed that was the unspoken bond between them—a streak of rebelliousness, and a total lack of enthusiasm for being here.

It was only Heather who made sure that Aurora never forgot her limitations, and openly ridiculed her for them. She didn't hesitate to inform Aurora sharply when she was following too closely on the trail, and sneered openly at Aurora's fear of bears, bees, fast-running creeks, and just about everything else they encountered. The almost instant dislike Aurora had felt from the other girl was not improved by the fact that they were forced to share a tent. Aurora had no experience at living in such close confines, and found it impossible to keep her things from spilling over on to Heather's side.

Heather also resented the fact Aurora had not—until now—been asked to pull her weight, and Aurora took a perverse kind of enjoyment in her resentment and played her role of the snotty rich girl to the hilt. It was her only edge after all—she would fall flat on her face trying to play the role of outdoor enthusiast extraordinaire.

And then there was Chance, who didn't openly show signs of disliking her, or of liking her, either. What was tough to swallow was that she found herself reluctantly respecting him—though her initial dislike was as strong as ever.

Still, Chance was a natural-born leader. Of that there was no doubt. He exuded a quality of quiet strength, decisiveness and authority, and even Aurora had to admit she trusted him. He knew what he was doing. His comfort and his confidence in the wilderness made her feel safe and secure even in this tremendously isolated area.

But it was more than knowledge that made people turn to him naturally for leadership and guidance. He handled the dozens of small crises—bound to occur when six people lived together in intense isolation and interdependence—with unshakable calm. Even the unexpected arrival of a beginner had given him only brief pause—his itineraries were quietly juggled to still give everyone the best possible trip.

Chance exuded the rare vitality of a man supremely sure of himself in the truest sense of the word. His own self-certainty seemed to bring out the best in others; he coaxed tremendous efforts from people, not for his own gain, but seemingly to instil them with confidence in their own capabilities. The fact that he liked people showed in the way he listened so intently to what was being said to him, and the fact that he liked his job showed in his tremendous, unflagging energy.

But he didn't like her. She was angrily aware that Chance's original estimation of her as selfish and spoiled had not changed. The charm and charisma he was capable of were rarely wasted on her. She was always aware that she was a nuisance in his eyes, and she went to great lengths to hide the respect she felt for him, letting only her dislike show. Since he was determined to dislike her anyway, dammit, she'd give him cause!

'I won't dig a latrine,' she repeated firmly.

'Hungry, princess?'

His lightning-swift change of subject put her on edge. She was famished. She ate with the appetite of three truckers out here and dinner always more than compensated for the quick, light fare provided for lunch.

The others all had a great deal of expertise in outdoor cooking, and she was constantly amazed by the gourmet creations that evolved out of the unappetising and uninspiring looking bags of dehydrated, freeze-dried, and powdered ingredients.

Suddenly the connection hit her. 'You can't possibly be threatening to send me to bed without supper!' she spluttered.

'It's not a threat, Aurora,' he said smoothly. 'I'm just presenting you with your choices. Either earn your keep, or don't get kept.'

She glared at him and her stomach growled mournfully.

'Aurora,' he said softly, 'on a streamlined trip like this, there's no room for deadweight. There are only six of us. There's nothing demeaning about doing your share. *I* pull duty like everybody else. I did the latrine yesterday; I'm cooking tonight.'

She saw immediately he was offering her an out with dignity, though she let not a flicker of her gratitude show in her face.

'Oh, all right,' she said grumpily. 'I suppose if Mr Macho himself can lower himself to cooking, a Fairhurst can lay hand to shovel. But hunger aside, I hope you burn whatever you make to a crisp and fall flat on your handsome face!'

She coloured feverishly at her slip of tongue, and beat a hasty retreat, but not hasty enough to escape his deep, rumbling chuckle.

He did not fall flat on his handsome face. He provided

a meal of fresh-caught Arctic grayling, perfectly sautéd in wild onions and butter. He collected the ingredients for a salad from the edible plant life in the area around the camp. The damned man had even cooked a wonderful light yeast bread over the coals of the fire, and then finished with a fruit cobbler made with dehydrated fruits and biscuit mix.

Oh well, it had been too much to hope for, Aurora thought, cleaning her plate with contented relish.

A squirrel blasted down an acorn missile at the intruders eating below his domain, and caught Scott squarely on the head. He yelped good-naturedly and grinned at Danny.

'How do you say squirrel in Stoney?' Scott asked him, knowing Chance was capitalising on the boy's fascination with the Indian culture to try and break down some of his barriers of hostility.

'Uh—pe-*zin*?' Danny shot Chance a hopeful look.

Chance pretended exasperation. 'No, me*tin*-oon, but at least you're in the right family. Pe-*zin* means gopher. Squirrel is see-*jah*.'

'And what's me*tin*-oon?' Heather asked, drawing a laugh because the word that came out of her mouth was nothing like the one that had come out of Chance's.

'Me*tin*-oon means little brother,' Chance explained, and Aurora caught Danny's look of surprised pleasure before it was savagely doused.

'How do you come to speak an Indian dialect, Chance?' Heather's tone dripped sweetness and sunshine, and Aurora barely contained her desire to roll her eyes.

'My interest stems from the fact my great-grandfather

was a Stoney Indian. That aspect of my heritage intrigues me, particularly in light of the pull I feel toward the wilderness. I feel he's a very strong part of me, somehow. To be able to know his culture and speak his language seems to bring me closer to myself.'

'Ain't life a bitch?' Danny's tough façade was back in place. 'You choose to live like a poor man, and the rest of us would give away our right arms for a week in that famous house——'

'That's enough.' Chance cut him off sharply. 'I've warned you about swearing before.'

But Aurora was watching him with keen interest. It wasn't the swearing that had hit a nerve. 'What house?' she asked innocently.

'Tell her,' Danny taunted, and Aurora could tell he despised himself for his earlier pleasure in Chance's use of an affectionate term. 'Why don't you tell her what Mr Chance Cody can go home to when he gets tired of playing Indian?'

'I said that was enough,' Chance repeated softly. 'I think we better have a little talk, hm?' He rose to his feet, and Aurora saw sudden wary fear in Danny's eyes before he shrugged carelessly and silently followed Chance out of the clearing.

'Goodnight,' she said into the awkward silence, getting up. She glanced in the direction Chance and Danny had gone, and hesitated. Surely that flash of fear in Danny's eyes had not been justified? He would probably only be embarrassed if she intervened.

She went and collected her soap and towel and made her way down to the creek, casting a furtive glance over her shoulder first. Chance insisted nobody use soap in the creek, even though the product was biodegradable. But tonight she felt a petty need to defy him, even if he would never know. It seemed to be taking things to a ridiculous extreme to haul a can of water away from the creek, anyway.

At the creek she soaped herself and then hurriedly washed off the soap with the bracing ice-cold glacial run-off.

'I've asked you not to use soap in the water, Aurora.'

As always, Chance had moved up behind her on incredibly silent feet, and she turned and glared at him, but the glare died and her eyes widened. Chance was shirtless, the towel draped around his neck brilliantly white against the deep, warm bronze of his chest. And what a chest, Aurora conceded with dismay. She had always thought hair curling on men's chests was rather sexy, and faintly enticing. Yet a hair on the smooth, hard surface of Chance's chest would have been sacrilege. How magnificent he was—the skin taut, satiny and unblemished over the corded muscles in his arms, over the broad expanse of his shoulders, over the rock-hard, well-cut definition of his breast and over the flat, hard surface of his stomach.

She turned from him abruptly, and it was partly to hide her powerful reaction to his naked torso that she said acidly, 'Don't be such a fanatic, Chance. I'm too tired to haul a can of water up higher.'

'I told you you don't really need to use soap. Plain cold water will get rid of any bacteria or odours.'

'Civilised people use soap!' she snapped, and then sighed. 'A little soap won't hurt your damned creek anyway. Nobody ever comes up here, so what does it matter? This creek is destined for oblivion. It could be no one will ever see it again. So what's a little soap?'

A silence followed her little speech, a silence much more unnerving than if Chance had lost his temper and snapped at her with contempt riding in his deep voice. When the silence stretched until her nerves were unreasonably taut, she broke it.

'How's Danny?' She looked accusingly over her shoulder at him. 'You didn't hurt him, did you?'

He looked startled, then he frowned. 'You seem to have this unflattering idea I hurt women and children.'

'Danny's not a child,' she reminded him.

'When you're thirty-five, sixteen isn't much better than a child—though don't ever tell Danny I said so. We just finished a discussion on behaving like a responsible adult.'

'Just a discussion?' she asked suspiciously.

'For God's sake, Aurora!'

'Well, he seemed frightened of you,' she defended herself, but smiled inwardly. She was just goading him. Dislike aside, she had been inwardly certain Chance would never hit Danny.

'Danny learned early that if he displeased people he would get the stuffing knocked out of him. In turn, he shows inappropriate displays of physical temper that get him into trouble. I'd hardly be doing my job if I got in on that vicious cycle.' He paused. 'Now, come here, Aurora.'

Mesmerised by deep, black eyes she put down her things and joined him, surprised when he took her hand and pulled her down beside him. It felt strangely good to be sitting beside Chance Cody, even if he had let go of her hand and now had his arms wrapped around his legs. Beware of his fatal charm, she cautioned herself.

'Wilderness Appreciation 101,' he announced softly. 'Close your eyes, Aurora.'

She glanced at him, and then quickly away. Why did this brief relapse from his customary remoteness make a glowing warmth begin deep in her belly? Beware, she reminded herself again before obediently closing her eyes.

'Listen,' he instructed softly. He waited a moment. 'What do you hear?'

'Nothing,' she said honestly. 'In fact, it's so quiet out here it nearly drives me crazy.'

She opened her eyes and looked at him again, and felt an absurd impulse to snuggle into the warm expanse of him, to wrap her arms around his naked waist, and lean her head against his chest. Instead she forced herself to move slightly further away from him, her spine stiff.

'Listen,' he said again, and she reclosed her eyes. 'It's not quiet at all. In fact it's quite noisy—it's just that you're used to a different kind of sound.'

Slowly, she came to understand what he meant. First, she became aware of the ever-present murmur of the creek, plopping and singing over rocks. And then she became aware of the gentle whisper of a faint breeze stirring the leaves and the branches of the trees. Birds calling and insects humming joined the symphony Chance was showing her how to hear.

A sensation of pure and childlike wonder wrapped itself around her—as if she had been deaf, and the gift of hearing was suddenly hers. As if she was strangely joined with and a part of the earth that sang so joyously around her. For the first time, she was glad she was here in this wilderness. For the first time, it occurred to her that if she wanted it to be, this trip could be more than an experience she had to suffer through in order to escape her father, Douglas, her world.

Her world? she thought mildly. At that moment, *this* world seemed like her world. The other seemed far away and long ago, and not quite real. The other seemed to be designed to keep Aurora Fairhurst from shining; to keep her locked away behind barriers and veneers and masks, a sad little princess encased in ritual and convention, imprisoned in a castle of ice.

She jerked her eyes open, feeling shaken, and oddly as if she had been sleeping when she knew she hadn't been. Chance's eyes were fastened on her face. Had they been the whole time? Why?

'What did you hear, princess?'

The word truth sprang into her mind, but she dismissed it. The decision she had come here to make had never, in her mind, included an evaluation of her lifestyle. She liked the fast lane—good parties, good clothes, fast cars. She liked being rich and relatively famous. Didn't she? The question she had come here to answer concerned only Douglas. Didn't it?

'Aurora?'

She looked at Chance. Why did she sometimes have the peculiar sensation he could read her heart? It would be ridiculous to believe he somehow knew she had just faced something painful. It would be even more ludicrous to believe that somewhere in this rough-edged stranger lurked a core of sensitivity that would help her to understand it.

'What are you running from?' The question was soft, and his perception shook her and seemed to confirm his ability to read her secrets.

The urge to tell him about her father and Douglas was overwhelmingly strong, but it faded quickly and was replaced with confusion. The stern mask, his unspoken censure, were gone. She had the uneasy feeling there was a side to this man she had not allowed herself to see because of their initial conflicts—that there was a side to this man she didn't want to see at all, because her dislike and her defensiveness made her safe somehow, safe and untouchable.

You, she wanted to say, I'm running away from you. Except that would be crazy for two reasons: one, she was running from her father, and two, if she was running from Chance she had forgotten to inform her feet and her fingers.

Because her feet didn't move, and her fingers did. Of their own volition they reached out and lingeringly traced the thick brow, the high proud cheekbone, the enticing line of his lips.

Shocked with herself, she snatched her hand away, her cheeks burning with mortification. 'I'm sorry—— I don't——'

'Shh,' he commanded, retrieving her hand, and brushing his lips across the knuckles. His eyes met hers, black and dancing, asking her a wordless question that she knew she had already answered.

'Chance,' she whispered once. She meant it as a protest. It sounded, instead, like a plea.

His lips closed over hers, and a moment that had been soft-focused and dreamy became electrically alive under the moist demanding pressure of his mouth.

For a moment she struggled with propriety, trying to recall her feelings of fervent dislike for this man. No, it wasn't even a moment. It was a weak flash that went out as quickly as a match snuffed in a mud puddle. Then her lips responded to his with the urgent hunger of a tigress too long caged, too long tamed.

Primal sensation enveloped her, wiping out all else, and she had no idea that what came to her instinctively could be mistaken for expertise, for invitation.

His kiss became bolder as her lips parted beneath his, and the caress of his tongue against hers, the brief brutal clash of his teeth against hers, sent fingers of liquid flame licking through her, lower and lower ...

His fingers, strong and sure, took up the throbbing tattoo that his lips had started. Featherlight they touched her earlobes, traced the column of her throat, dealt with her buttons with swift confidence, and then forged an unerring path over her trembling stomach, over her ribcage, to her heaving breast.

A gentleness suddenly muted his urgency as he unfastened the front clasp on her bra.

Perhaps it was the change in mood that she sensed, or perhaps it was his total ease with the bra fastening, but it threw her back into reality with the brutal force of a tiny boat being smashed against rocks by a storm-tossed sea.

'No!' She jerked away from him, her eyes full of accusation. This was the man who could identify Shalimar at twenty paces, who had casually forewarned her of his philosophies on life and lust!

'God,' she murmured, looking hastily down at her buttons, and fastening them with fingers made shaky with shame and humiliation. She had let him—just as he had predicted she would.

'I must say I didn't really expect the outraged virgin act from you.' His voice was dry, and she found it painfully composed.

She stared at him, stung. Surely to God she didn't give off the signals of a woman who played fast and loose? Of course she didn't, she told herself heatedly. If anything she came across as an ice maiden, a fact the rejected swains at the country club had occasionally passed on to her with some eagerness after she had effectively snubbed them.

But the country club was a long time ago, and far away, a fact she was uncomfortably aware of for the second time tonight.

'Maybe I am an outraged virgin,' she said with a weak attempt at lightness that sounded pathetically tentative and strained.

Chance's expression was nothing less than scornful, and she felt an agonising sense of loss that she dearly wanted to deny.

'Aurora, save the higher classes' carefully engineered morality myth for the fools who want to believe in the fairytales that your press agents weave for them. But I've been there, and I don't have any Cinderella illusions left.'

'Isn't it a form of reverse discrimination to believe that everyone in a certain income bracket behaves a certain way?' she snapped coldly. 'I have yet to make the cover of the *Enquirer* for my wild and wicked ways.'

'Well, your unhappy marriage to what's-his-face should help you make up for lost time.'

'His name is Douglas, and we won't be unhappy!' She wished she sounded more convinced. For some reason she also wished, almost desperately, that she could convince him that what he wanted to believe wasn't true. But she didn't even attempt it. It was naïve to expect him ever to like or respect her.

'I'm going to bed,' she said in a clipped, strangled tone.

'I think that's a good idea,' he responded and she thought she detected weariness in his tone, and looked sharply at him. But no, there was no weariness in that shadowed face; no nothing, the expression remote, the eyes as flat and as unreadable as black ice.

She moved away, but then made the mistake of looking back. Impotent rage boiled in her throat.

'Barbarian,' Aurora spat at him.

He didn't look back.

'Would you be kind enough to keep your junk on your own side of the tent?'

Aurora had only just put her head through the door, and she looked at Heather helplessly. All she wanted was to be back home in her own safe world where people had finesse and reserve and the decency to hide their lusty selves behind a lovely set of social graces.

Heather was watching her narrowly. 'Where have you been? You're never awake at this time of night.'

'I was at the creek,' Aurora said woodenly.

'Alone?'

'No.' Aurora pulled her shirt over her head. 'Chance was there.'

Heather's gaze narrowed even more. 'I wouldn't get

any ideas, if I were you. It's perfectly clear that Chance isn't your type.'

'Perfectly clear,' Aurora agreed coldly, though somehow her uncaring tone wasn't as accurate a reflection of her feelings as she would have liked. She crawled into her sleeping bag, and closed her eyes.

A terrible sound suddenly split the air, and Aurora, her nerves taut anyway, sat up, her eyes wide with fear. 'What was that?'

'What?' Heather asked impatiently, as the sound echoed eerily through the night again.

'Don't you hear it? It sounds like there are hillbillies around here who have been drinking. They're shrieking and cackling. Heather, you must be able to hear them!' Aurora had never heard such a hair-raising noise in all her life, and she was sure only those driven insane were capable of making it. 'Oh, God,' she moaned, 'do you suppose they'll kill us?'

'Oh, shut up, Aurora. "They" are coyotes. They've been at it every night, while the poor, exhausted socialite who is wrecking everybody's trip caught up on her beauty rest, I suppose.'

Aurora dismissed the barbs, unable to summon her normal tone of haughtiness. 'Do they kill people?' she asked nervously.

'No!' Heather snapped. 'But I might.' Then she chuckled with smug satisfaction. 'No, you, my girl, are most certainly not Chance's type.'

'Who on earth would want to be?' Aurora shot back with convincing disdain, then turned abruptly on her side, and pretended instant sleep.

But sleep was far from instant in coming. She wanted

to dismiss Chance from her tortured mind, and couldn't. Instead she found herself going over and over the pieces of him that she had discovered today, manipulating and twisting them to try and fit them into a mental jigsaw puzzle.

The famous house, a vague connection with Robards, what she had to assume was a basic familiarity with the ballet, a turn of phrase that suggested a good education ... and finally, from his own mouth, his stinging statement that he had 'been there'.

There. Her world. His world, too? It seemed absurd, and yet suddenly a picture formed in her mind of Chance Cody, elegant in a dinner jacket, looking suave and self-assured and powerful. Powerful in more than the physical sense of the word—powerful in the way of men who commanded empires and other people's respect.

And yet, even trapped within stiff formal wear, Chance would be untouched. He would somehow be carrying his wilderness deep within him. Carrying within him an ancestry of strength, of pride, and of dignity.

But he would fit in her world. Of that she was certain. She was less certain he would want to. In fact, she could picture him standing on the edge of a crowded room, taking in the glitter, and stopping hearts with the contemptuous sweep of his warrior eyes.

CHAPTER FIVE

'THE hooch-crazed hillbillies didn't get you last night, Aurora?'

Aurora, arranging her pack for the day, turned and treated Danny to a frosty look. Heather had lost no time in telling the whole camp, she thought bitterly, and now she'd be a laughing stock! Well, she wouldn't give anybody the satisfaction of thinking it bothered her.

She lifted her chin haughtily, meeting Danny's eyes with icy uncaring. His grey eyes were dancing with mischief, and certainly with amusement, but with sudden insight she realised he wasn't laughing at her. Even his normal quota of cynicism was not present in his expression.

Why, he's teasing me, she guessed, surprised and oddly delighted. As the only child of aloof parents, teasing fell out of the realm of her experience, though suddenly she could remember visiting days at boarding school and watching a few of the girls with older brothers and fathers who playfully baited them. She could remember a wistful sensation of envy at the warmth and fun she had glimpsed in some other people's families.

'How do you say hillbilly in Stoney?' she teased back, poker-faced, and then grinned. Danny laughed, and watched her close her pack, and slip it on.

'Hey, Aurora, you're starting to do that like a real pro.'

'Am I?' she asked, startled and pleased by the casual compliment. I wonder if Chance thinks so, she wondered, and then felt angry with herself. Who cared what Chance thought? And he wasn't likely to notice how she put on her pack anyway. This morning at breakfast he had said a cool good morning to her, and then become engrossed in a conversation with Heather, making Aurora feel very near invisible. She told herself she didn't care, and yet she felt a seething kind of rage when she saw his black head bent close to Heather's, when she saw the flash of the smile that was not, and probably never again would be, directed at her.

I'm jealous, she had thought with dismay, and then been chagrined with herself. Jealous, indeed! It was not possible to be jealous of someone you detested! So what if last night for a few wonderfully magic moments he had seemed sensitive and capable of compassion? So what if last night it seemed as if there was a depth to Chance it would take a lifetime to explore? So what, if the touch of his lips had carried her to a dizzying height that she doubted she would ever recapture? The bitter ending to their rendezvous was fair warning of his true nature, a nature as hard and wild—a heart as untamable—as that of his ancestor.

Her eyes had inadvertently sought out the object of her mullings, and she became aware of Danny following her gaze thoughtfully. She looked hastily away from Chance, unable to prevent the faint blush from rising in her cheeks as she looked defiantly at Danny, daring him to draw the wrong conclusions.

Danny was unintimidated by her challenging glare.

'Too late. I saw it,' he said, watching her face wickedly. 'But I knew before. You two are kind of alike. It's more than you both being——' He stopped abruptly and looked uncomfortable, and Aurora realised he had been warned to keep his mouth shut about Chance's background. 'I just feel something between you,' he finished awkwardly.

'It's called intense dislike,' Aurora snapped. 'Chance is the kind of man I despise. He's arrogant and egotistical and domineering, and I can't remember when I've felt such complete aversion for another human being!'

'Wow,' Danny commented happily, 'you've got it bad.'

'I've got nothing "bad",' she denied heatedly.

Danny shrugged patronisingly. 'Whatever you say. Ain't no skin off my nose.'

'In case you haven't noticed, I happen to be engaged,' Aurora informed him stiffly.

'Hard to miss a ring that size,' Danny said wryly, 'but that don't mean nothing. A friend of my sister's was engaged three times before she finally took the long walk.' He hesitated, obviously struggling with something.

'Ever heard of Claire Bartek?' he finally asked carelessly.

Funny he should mention that name, Aurora thought, when just last night she had made reference to the rich young women whose names were splashed across the front pages of the gutter press. Not that Claire was so young any more, though she was still as wildly lovely as she had ever been. Would there be anybody who didn't recognise that enormously rich and naughty woman's name? She was a case for engagements not being carved in stone—she had nearly a dozen of those to her credit—and at thirty-two she was already on husband number three. Rumours of a lover abounded.

Danny looked over his shoulder guiltily. 'My cousin says Chance was engaged to her, a long time ago.'

'To Claire Bartek?' Aurora asked, her voice rising incredulously.

Danny looked like he wanted to clamp his hand over her mouth. 'Don't ever say you heard it from me,' he hissed.

'I won't,' she promised, her mind whirling. Her eyes trailed to where Chance stood supervising the camp break up. Poor Chance, she thought, a thought inconsistent with the power and confidence he radiated. Poor me, she added, as another piece of his puzzle slipped into place. No wonder he had such an aversion to her; no wonder he had jumped to an entirely unfair conclusion last night. If he had really been engaged to Claire Bartek, he had undergone the test of fire as far as spoiled and wealthy women were concerned—no wonder he was cynical and scarred.

Against her will, her mind drifted to Claire Bartek. Aurora had been a child when she had seen her at a charity function, and she had been entranced. She had never seen such perfection—such an exquisite face, such gorgeous clothes clinging to a body that was full-figured without the slightest tendency toward fat. Claire Bartek was perfection right down to the amused light that glowed in those famous soft-suede eyes, the delightful husky note in her voice, the tinkle of her laughter.

It had been a brief meeting, quickly forgotten, except when Claire's lovely face graced the front pages of various disreputable magazines—which it did with some frequency. And then Aurora would feel briefly disenchanted with the woman whose beauty went only skin deep, whose charm was affected, and artificial. There was something about Claire Bartek that made her sad.

Where had this woman fitted into Chance's life? Had she loved him? Was she even capable of love? Had he loved her? Did those incredible doe eyes have something to do with the fact that Chance had never married?

For a reason she didn't care to explore, the thought of Chance loving someone filled her with an aching sense of wistfulness. What would it be like to be the one that rugged, fierce face softened for? To be the one who brought tender warmth out in icy black eyes? What would it be like to be the one to lie in the circle of those powerful arms, sharing hopes and dreams, exploring together the mysteries and miracles of the universe, the mysteries and miracles of a man and a woman? Dismayed with her wayward thoughts, she hurriedly made her way to join the other hikers.

Feeling released from physical strain for the first time, she was able to appreciate the magnificent, overpowering beauty around her. Some time last night, she realised slowly, she had made a decision to enjoy her surroundings and now they opened up for her like a sparkling jewel in a freshly opened box. She noticed the intense azure of the sky, the brilliant white of snow on the mountain tops, the million shades of green in the dense forest. She noticed the sounds that emerged above the hush—insects croaking, birds singing, leaves whispering against one another. The very air seemed to tingle with a fresh, crisp vibrancy all its own.

Despite that aggravating conversation with Danny this morning, despite the brutal conclusion of her conversation with Chance last night, she felt strangely contented, almost as if the muted, tranquil green of the forest was seeping into her soul. The wilderness almost mocked human complexities. What are you among this? she could hear it whispering to her.

At lunch she found a log, and happily planted herself on it, munching on crackers liberally spread with cheese, and followed by 'gorp', a high energy mix of nuts and raisins laced generously with M&Ms.

'You've got the best seat in the house. Can we join you?'

Aurora glanced up at the freckle-faced twins. 'Free world,' she shrugged.

Hank raised an eyebrow at Scott. 'Did that sound snooty to you?'

'Very snooty,' Scott agreed soberly. 'I vote we push her off the log and have it for ourselves.'

Aurora was startled by this response to her habitual put-down to young men who wanted to join her—young men who invariably knew who she was, and whose interest she never quite trusted. But this wasn't a restaurant table or an empty lounger beside the pool, and it was impossible to suspect Hank and Scott of ulterior motives in seeking her company.

Aurora giggled as the boys moved slowly toward her, trying to make their guileless faces look menacing.

'It was snooty!' She choked her admission through

laughter. 'And I'm sorry. You can share. I'd be honoured——'

Too late! A twin firmly gripped each arm, and gently tossed her off the log, settling themselves in the place where she had been.

She chortled with laughter. She was being teased again, she realised, and it was almost like being a member of a family. It gave her a warm sense of belonging that didn't quite compare to anything she had ever felt before . . . that her own children might never feel, she thought with unexpected sombreness, if she married Douglas. Her own life would just repeat itself. Could she really say she wouldn't give in to pressure to send her children to boarding school, or hire one of those indispensable British nannies? Even if she did win that battle did she want her children to have a father who was never there? Who was so wrapped up in the intrigues of his business that he would try to make up for his lack of interest in his family with expensive gifts?

It occurred to her that she had never thought of Douglas in terms of his being a father. Or herself in terms of being a mother. Wasn't it odd for two people who were planning marriage not to discuss something as important as parenthood? Wasn't it odd that she had never imagined what it would feel like to have a small, black-eyed baby nuzzled against her breast?

Douglas doesn't have black eyes, a small voice informed her cheerfully.

Oh, hell, she thought, dismissing the split-second thoughts, and scrambling to her feet. 'This looks like the best seat in the house,' she said, with exaggerated contriteness. 'Will you share it?'

'Free world,' the twins chorused, and then slipped apart so that she could sit right in between them. They ate their lunch shoulder to shoulder, the twins revealing natures as guileless as their faces. How different they were, Aurora mused, from the young people at the country club. There was none of that faint boredom edging their voices and their eyes, nothing either pretentious or sophisticated in their stories or their mannerisms. She found herself laughing helplessly at their 'twin' tales about switching classes and girlfriends and jobs for amusement and plain devilment.

Chance came over and regarded their laughter-flushed faces without humour, and for some reason they all shut up, looking at him like children who had been caught with their hands in the biscuit tin.

'Aurora, you'll be cooking dinner tonight,' he bit out, and walked away.

They stared after him.

'Wow, what's got into him?' Hank whistled. 'If looks could kill, I think the three of us would be pushing up daisies.'

'Chance Cody has no sense of humour,' Aurora informed them sourly.

Both young men looked at her with surprise.

'That isn't so, Aurora,' Hank said, looking at Aurora thoughtfully. His brow puckered, he gazed after Chance. 'I think he's jealous,' he deduced softly.

Aurora was stunned. It was the second time in one day that it had been insinuated that Chance felt something for her beyond the disdain he allowed her to see. Were she and Chance really sending a message—albeit a stormy one—that everybody else was receiving loud and clear, but to which they were deaf and dumb themselves? She remembered the passion of their encounter last night and her heart did a hopeful little flip-flop, which she got firmly under control.

Why did she always become a person divided where Chance was concerned? she moaned inwardly. The sane part of her refused to give in to her attraction to him, and was almost able to refuse to admit it even existed. And yet another part—another part as wild and untamed as Chance himself was—insisted on feeling something very different for the powerful, self-assured man. Was Chance caught up in the same quandary? It was evident—embarrassingly so—that the mysterious undercurrents between them were being picked up by others.

'She's blushing!' Scott crowed with delight.

'I am not!' And I am also not cooking any damned dinner tonight, she vowed to herself.

'Let's move out!' Chance called, his voice as hard and cold as that of a drill sergeant.

Aurora walked along the trail contemplating her options. Digging a latrine or sump hole or contributing to camp clean-up was one thing. Cooking was quite another. She had no intention of cooking dinner. She would look like a complete fool trying to match her non-existent skills against those of the outdoor gourmets all around her. Chance had probably figured that out, she assumed angrily, and he was probably delighting in placing her in a predicament that she was totally alien to and uncomfortable with. Golly, Mindy had said this trip was worth a small fortune. The least Chance could have done was brought a cook along! Why should she do it? She'd simply trade jobs with Scott or Hank for the evening, and if Chance didn't like it, that was too bad, she told herself rebelliously. That would show him not everybody leapt to do his bidding and win his favour—and particularly not her!

'Aurora, I don't think Chance would like that,' Scott commented after she'd offered to change jobs with him.

'It doesn't have a thing to do with Chance.' Aurora returned irritably. 'Mr High-and-Mighty's stamp of approval doesn't have to go on every little thing, does it? Besides, I can't cook. I've never so much as plugged in a toaster.'

'Well, maybe you should tell *him* that,' Scott said doubtfully.

'Forget it then. If you're not man enough to make a decision all by yourself, I'll ask Danny.'

'That was below the belt, Aurora,' Scott said softly, dignity and hurt mixed in his face.

Aurora felt an unexpected stab of pain. He'd never been anything but nice to her, and she repaid him with a put-down. She had always been rather proud of the fact she was a master of the put-down and that she could skilfully use disdain to manipulate people to do what she wanted them to do. That was perfectly acceptable in her crowd—in fact an acid tongue could be quite admired. Suddenly it seemed so petty and ugly, just another game that kept her in a cage, rather than letting her out.

Maybe, she admitted woefully, Chance wasn't so far wrong in his assessment of her as selfish and spoiled. She sighed heavily.

'Scott, I should have never asked you and I'm sorry.'

She looked glumly at her toes. 'I just hate looking like a fool, and as far as this group goes, I'm already the worst at everything.'

'Nobody thinks like that, Aurora,' Scott said gently. He looked at her distressed face, and grinned reluctantly. 'OK, I'll cook for you. But because we're friends, and because all Danny can cook is macaroni and cheese, not because you challenged my manhood.'

He regarded her thoughtfully and then continued softly, 'You know, Aurora, the role of rich bitch doesn't really suit you. Maybe you should quit trying so hard to be something you aren't.'

'Well, if I'm not that, then what am I?' she asked with forced lightness.

'I think you've been letting other people answer that question for you for far too long.' Scott turned and walked away.

She felt like she had just been told—very gently—to grow up.

'What do you think you're doing?'

Aurora was unable to prevent herself from jumping at the sound of that voice so close to her ear.

'I think I'm building a sump hole,' she said innocently. 'In fact, I could almost swear that's what I'm doing.'

'Oh. I had this funny idea it was your turn to cook tonight. Should I check my list just to make sure I'm not mixed up?'

She bridled under the sarcasm. 'As a matter of fact, I switched jobs with Scott.'

'As a matter of fact, that's against the rules,' he drawled easily.

'It's a free country, and I think Scott and I can both be considered adult enough to make a few tiny decisions for ourselves.'

'The jobs rotate, Aurora. Everybody tries everything. Consider it my humble attempt to provide a well-rounded education.'

'How very altruistic of you, Chance,' she said sweetly, 'but I have to refuse your kind consideration. I don't cook.'

'Don't or can't?' he asked with soft perception.

'Don't, can't, won't.' She tossed her hair with brave defiance.

He looked at her closely, and suddenly she saw the faintest of changes in his expression, some of the sternness melting, the eyes holding a subtle light of totally unappreciated and unwanted sympathy.

'Aurora,' he said patiently, and almost gently, 'all you had to do was ask for help if it embarrassed you that you don't know how to cook.'

'It doesn't embarrass me,' she denied furiously. 'It just doesn't interest me either!'

He seemed to be seeing through her, and the gentleness did not disappear from his tone. 'How do you know that?'

She ducked her head, and looked at her feet, unable to meet that look in his eyes any longer. Don't, Chance, she pleaded inwardly. Threaten me, be mad at me, be cruel, be indifferent, but don't look at me so gently—please.

'I just know,' she stammered.

A strong hand came under her chin, and against her will her eyes were lifted to his. 'You must have had one or two cooking classes along the way,' he probed quietly.

Aurora shook her head. 'I skipped them. And gym.'

Chance sighed, and released her chin. 'OK,' he said, 'my mistake.' Aurora felt enormous relief. Unfortunately, it didn't last long.

'I still want you to cook,' he said firmly.

'No!'

'Aurora, how many things are you going to be willing to pass up in this life because you're afraid of failing or of being embarrassed? You're setting yourself up for one dull life. Living—really living—requires some risks.'

'I'm not cooking,' she flared, but it took effort, and it was only to goad Chance into being the savage, cruel man who was so easy to hate. They were still too close to that kiss of last night for her to want to see that compelling and compassionate side of his nature again. It was too dangerous. Oh, God, she thought with despair, how right he is. Even my heart is ruled by my fear that I'm going to make a mistake and end up embarrassed, or hurt. I deserve Douglas, and dullness. I deserve never to know what it would be like to be loved by a man like this.

He refused to be goaded, though his voice was firm. 'Fine, Aurora, don't cook. I can't very well force you to, though I suspect that's what you want, isn't it? You'd love me to prove that I'm every bit the barbarian you're convinced I am—to threaten you with violence or to shake you till your teeth rattle. You'll find this difficult to believe, I'm sure, but I've never touched a woman in anger in my entire life, and I don't believe in using physical superiority to convince people to see things my way.

'But, Aurora, nobody is cooking for you. It's not

Scott's turn to cook or Heather's, Danny's or mine. So if you don't want to cook, nobody eats. No one is going to look after *your* responsibility for you. Maybe it's about time you learned there's a price to be paid for always wanting your own way at everyone else's expense. Teamwork is based on everybody doing their part—and if you're not willing to do that, the rest of the team is going to suffer. This time, we miss a hot meal, which is no big deal. I'm sure everyone will survive. But maybe next time survival *will* be threatened. If you can't practise teamwork in the little things, you'll find it sadly lacking when you attempt the big things.'

Aurora was silent for a long time, knowing herself to be well and truly beaten. 'I guess,' she finally said weakly, 'I could try cooking—though I think you'll be sorry.' She glanced up into his face, bracing herself to see the black eyes smug with mockery at his easy victory over her.

Instead, she was surprised to see a warm smile playing across his lips. 'Welcome to Chef Cody's School of Cooking,' he said easily.

Chance helped her collect some wild plants for a salad, and then went through a dog-eared recipe book with her, suggesting good choices for a beginner. With an encouraging, somewhat brotherly slap on her shoulder, he left her on her own. For a moment she looked helplessly at the ingredients in front of her, sorely tempted to blow it on purpose so that nobody would ever ask her to cook again.

But she recognised her reaction not as rebelliousness, but as fear of being humiliated, and she could hear

Chance daring her to learn to live to the fullest by risking. This was such a small risk; if she couldn't rise to this challenge, could she ever rise to any other? She thought of dark eyes that filled her with a strange fear, too, and suddenly conquering fear was a challenge she couldn't walk away from. She flung herself into preparing her meal with vigour.

It hadn't been much, she thought contentedly, a little over an hour later. A salad, a rice and cheese casserole, some biscuits, and a water-based chocolate pudding. The salad, made with the tender leaves of the saxifrage plant and wild onions, then doused liberally with oil and vinegar, had been excellent. The casserole was passable, the biscuits burned beyond edibility, and the pudding lumpy.

And yet she felt a ridiculous sense of pride in her efforts. With the exception of Heather, everybody complimented her and in some way she felt they shared her pride. It was as if by accepting this small challenge she had earned a stripe—her right to become a full-fledged member of this group. *Trying*, she remembered Chance saying the first day, *was as good as a goal*, and that's how he and Scott and even Danny had made her feel—like she had scored a goal, for herself.

Why, she wondered, did her parents think it was such a privilege not to have to do things for themselves? She was beginning to think a good measure of self-sufficiency might have done—might still do—her the world of good.

The dishes were being done when Chance approached her, and smiled down at her flushed face. 'I'm proud of you, Aurora,' he told her quietly.

She shrugged, quickly concentrating on another soapy plate, but at that moment she felt as if she could go to the edges of the earth if Chance Cody asked her to.

'Hey, Aurora,' Scott called, as she put the last plate away, 'come on. Hank and Danny and I have found a use for your biscuits. We're going to play a little catch. What about you, Chance? Heather?'

Heather smiled indulgently at the twins. 'Chance and I are going for a walk,' she cooed.

Aurora willed herself to study a broken fingernail, but out of the corner of her eye she saw Chance and Heather rise, Chance throwing his arm companionably around Heather's shoulder as they moved away.

She refused to look after them, her face a mask of indifference even while her mind whirled painfully. She had seen Chance at his best as a leader when he had talked to her before dinner. He had managed to put aside his personal feelings, used all the strength and charm of his character to make her see things his way. It wasn't really his fault that she had read more into it than he ever intended. It wasn't really his fault that she had believed he had changed his mind about her, that he was willing to admit maybe that she wasn't as much spoiled and selfish and shallow, as sheltered and uncertain and fearful.

It wasn't Chance's fault that he had forgotten to tell her that risking sometimes left people more vulnerable to pain, and to human hurt, than they had ever allowed themselves to be before.

'Aurora, are you playing ball?'

'I don't play ball,' she said stiffly, 'and I don't want to learn.' She turned and walked away, with her head high.

Was Chance going to kiss Heather as he had kissed her? Had Claire Bartek succeeded in making him such a cynic that one woman was totally interchangeable with another?

'I don't care what he does,' she muttered fiercely. But there was another voice. Please don't kiss her, it whimpered pleadingly, please.

CHAPTER SIX

HEATHER came into the tent late that night, making no attempt not to awaken her tentmate. Aurora, who had been sleeping fitfully anyway, opened her eyes and noticed it was fairly dark for the first time in her experience in the Yukon.

Heather, seeing she was awake, smiled smugly at her. 'Chance and I watched a sub-arctic sunset together.'

'Goody for you,' Aurora said coldly, and turned on her side. *Did he kiss her?*

'It was so incredibly beautiful,' Heather contined. 'The sky darkens and darkens and darkens to kind of a deep twilight, and the sun kind of wallows, and then dips and starts to come up again. It was terribly romantic.'

'Am I supposed to care?' Aurora muttered grouchily. *Did he kiss her?*

'Oh,' Heather breathed dreamily, as if she had not heard Aurora's discouraging remark, 'I think I'm in love.'

He had kissed her. Aurora felt her heart drop, and then she turned and looked at Heather. 'That's stupid. You can't fall in love in four days.' Oh? a voice inside her taunted. Can't you? Isn't it possible to lose your heart in four seconds, never mind four days? It is not, Aurora answered herself primly.

'It was that fast with Don, too,' Heather said, almost absently, a slight unconscious frown creasing her brow.

'Who is Don?' Aurora had to ask, for all that she wanted to pretend total indifference to Heather's private life.

'My husband. My ex-husband. Well, not quite my ex-husband. We're separated.'

The statement was made airily, but Aurora sensed the airiness had been practised, and detected a faint bitter hurt behind it. Sensitivity to undertones had never exactly been her forte and she was a little surprised with herself, and even more surprised at her genuine sympathy for her cantankerous tentmate.

'I'm sorry,' Aurora said.

'Nothing to be sorry about,' Heather rebuffed her sharply. 'People do grow apart, develop different tastes. I didn't think it was fun any more, either. I was bored, too.'

The words gave away more than Heather probably wanted them to, Aurora thought. Her husband had obviously left her, and Aurora sensed Heather was weakly echoing the excuses Don had given her—developing 'different tastes': a sad euphemism for having found somebody new.

Aurora suspected Heather's new found love of Chance didn't go very deep. It was probably a way of showing Don she could develop 'different tastes', too, a way of proving to herself that she was still attractive and a way of rebuilding the confidence that must have been badly shattered.

Heather slanted Aurora a narrow look, as if she had guessed the sincerity of what she felt for Chance was being silently questioned. 'I knew right away that you weren't his type at all. But still, I thought you were rather striking, in a way that seems to appeal to men, no matter how rugged they are themselves. But then you washed your face off, and you're not really very striking at all, and I'm sure Chance doesn't think so, either.'

Aurora managed to prevent herself from wincing, but barely. She had been hit in a soft spot, and she momentarily would have killed to get her hands on her cosmetics kit—bears or no. But, looking at Heather, it suddenly struck her that the other girl wouldn't have made a catty remark like that unless she was a little uncertain about Aurora's ability to attract Chance—a little uncertain about what Chance really felt for Aurora, or Aurora for him.

Well, Aurora thought waspishly, you might as well join the whole camp, including me, in wondering about that one, Heather.

Refusing to rise or respond to the little digs, she smiled sweetly, and with an outward show of unperturbed confidence. 'Goodnight, Heather.' She closed her eyes, but not before she saw Heather narrow her eyes and look at her with intense dislike.

Though she had got Heather's goat by refusing to admit that her confidence relied in any way on her looks, Aurora was up early the following morning. In a little stand of trees behind her tent she fished a small compact out of her pocket and viewed her reflection critically for the first time in days. How could a girl who never spent less than an hour in front of the mirror in the mornings have so quickly and blithely dismissed her looks for the past few days? She hadn't really given a thought to what she looked like, until now.

Now she saw two distinctly lopsided braids with rebellious little strands of hair jutting out all over the place. Her face was wind and sunburned and the freckles across her nose had not only darkened, but increased in number. Her eyes looked round and childlike and she was sporting a mosquito bite on the end of her nose. There was not the least hint of hard-earned worldly sophistication in her face.

'I've never looked so terrible in my entire life!' she moaned with shattered dismay.

'You look great.'

'How dare you sneak up on me!' She whirled to see Hank standing behind her.

'Aw, Aurora, I didn't sneak up on you. A moose could have come crashing through the woods and you wouldn't have noticed, you were so engrossed in your mug.'

She was not thrilled with his choice of terms.

'You do look great,' he assured her seriously. 'All that gloop on your face just made you seem untouchable, somehow. Too glossy and artificial. I like the way you look now—kind of fresh and open and real. Kind of like the girl next door.'

'Yuk!' Aurora bit out vehemently.

'No, it's nice, Aurora. Your other face seemed like a bad fit somehow.'

Just like my other life. The renegade thought popped into her head before she could stop it.

'Me and Scott have this theory, anyway, that women goop up their faces for each other. I don't think men notice, unless they kind of wonder why on earth anybody would want purple eyelids.'

'Thank you for enlightening me,' she said stiffly, and then an outlaw giggle slipped by her defenses. 'I have to admit I've occasionally wondered about that myself—purple eyelids, I mean.'

Hank grinned. 'All I'm trying to say is don't worry about it, Aurora. It's too beautiful up here to be self-involved. You got a whole lot more going for you than your looks, anyway.'

She could feel his genuine affection and was absurdly moved by it. 'Thank you, Hank.'

He gave her a courtly bow and moved off, leaving her to look thoughtfully after him. It wasn't that she wasn't used to being liked, but she was always slightly cynical of the reasons people liked her. Sometimes she knew without a doubt it was because she represented a vast fortune, other times she thought it was because she worked so hard to 'fit'; to always do and say the right things that ensured membership in the right circles; to always look the 'right' way. When she thought about it, she couldn't even be sure that Douglas felt any genuine liking for her. She possessed the correct lineage, and social graces, but did he like her? As the people up here liked her?

The people here were seeing her at her very worst, where she couldn't do anything 'right', and they seemed to care about her anyway. For some reason that took a bit of the sting out of the face she had just confronted in the mirror and out of the grim realisation that she was considering marrying a man who was as much a stranger to her as she was to him.

After breakfast, she found a quiet place to load her pack. She didn't want to be anywhere near Heather, who was still waxing poetic about the midnight sun, though Aurora had noticed with some satisfaction that Chance didn't add his personal comments about the experience.

'Hey, Rory!'

At first, Aurora ignored the call, the possibility that *she* was being addressed never even occurring to her. And when it did her whole back stiffened with righteous indignation. It seemed to underline everything Heather had said about Chance not finding her attractive. 'Rory' was certainly not how one addressed an attractive woman! She was willing to bet he had never called Claire Bartek 'Bart'.

Chance was beside her, and Aurora glared up at him. Her wisdom of moments ago—her certainty that beauty was more than skin deep—had been fleeting. Now she felt self-conscious and very aware of her bedraggled appearance, and very resentful of the way he looked. Despite the primitive conditions, Chance looked extremely well-groomed, tanned, healthy, and infinitely at home with himself.

'Don't call me Rory,' she warned him imperiously.

He returned her gaze easily, faint mischief dancing in his black eyes. 'Why not?'

'Because I don't like it! I don't like pet names. And it's—it's a boy's name.

A light like a smouldering flame licked at his eyes. His gaze moved down her lazily and impertinently, flicking the swell of her breast with heat so intense she felt burned.

'Your name could be Chuck and you'd be in no danger of being mistaken for a boy, Aurora,' he chided her softly, his eyes returning to her face, wicked amusement dancing with a hint of challenge in their depths. 'Why don't you like pet names?'

That black gaze flicked to her engagement ring, and darkened, the amusement suddenly erased from his face. 'Doesn't *he* call you one? Doesn't he call you Rory, or little love, or darling or sweetheart? Doesn't he have a name for you that's all his own, that he whispers to you in the darkness when he holds you to him?'

'He doesn't——' She stopped, flushing. She decided, too late, that she didn't want Chance to know that Douglas didn't have a pet name for her, didn't whisper to her, certainly didn't hold her in the darkness.

Chance's eyes seemed to be looking right into her soul, and she saw an unfathomable anger flicker in them.

'What kind of man is he?' Chance demanded with soft, dangerous intensity. 'What the hell has he done to make you doubt your own femininity?' He paused. 'Or is it what he hasn't done?' he said slowly, a note of incredulous disbelief in his voice.

For a moment her heart skyrocketed at the implication that Chance found her irresistibly attractive, and that he could be so utterly disbelieving that another man could be indifferent to her charms. But how flattering was that? How flattering was an animal attraction, a purely chemical reaction not based on love or respect? Oh, it was strong, she had to admit that, dangerously, overwhelmingly strong. But it wasn't enough, for all that it would be tempting to surrender to the mysterious, nearly electrical force that snapped and crackled in the air between them.

She beat a hasty retreat from the almost tangible

danger in the air, seeking refuge in her engagement. 'Douglas isn't very demonstrative, and neither am I,' she said stiffly. 'We love each other for different qualities.'

'Love?' Chance hissed. He was silent for a long moment, and when he spoke his voice was soft, and contemplative. 'he doesn't love you. And you don't love him. You, not demonstrative, Rory? Don't make me laugh. Everything from the spark in your eyes to the way you walk screams a passionate nature. You're going to marry somebody who murders that? Why?'

She didn't answer, and his eyes narrowed. 'Oh, I see. He meets with the Fairhurst family approval, doesn't he, Aurora? What's his last name? No, don't tell me. I'm sure I can guess—Smithton or Filling or Emery——'

'Chance, stop it,' she pleaded. It was only the truth. Why did she feel cut to the quick that he had recognised it?

'You know that bothers me the most, Aurora? It's that you would think so little of yourself that you'd allow yourself to be used like that.'

'Used?' she stammered. No . . . Sven had used her as a route to her money, but Douglas had his own money. But sickly she remembered her own conclusions about Douglas this morning. They were virtually strangers. He didn't really care about her and never had. Oh, the way he was using her was more subtle, and this time with parental approval instead of without it, but he was still only using her. It was still the Fairhurst name he wanted, the Fairhurst name he was marrying. Hadn't she always really know that Douglas didn't so much like her for herself, as for what she could do for him?

Suddenly she saw Douglas Hartman for exactly what

he was—a man just like her father, who had analytically placed ambition above personal feelings. Behind that smooth, charming mask it was even possible he dreaded the thought of marrying her, but was willing to pay that price.

Sven. Douglas. Her father. Was she ever going to know a man who could love her for herself? Or was she somehow flawed? Totally unlovable?

Chance was watching her closely, his eyes narrowed. He seemed to sense her defeat and her sadness, and his hands suddenly locked around her wrists, and she was jerked to her feet. With animal swiftness that there was no avoiding, one hand was locked on the small of her back, the other pressed into her neck, ensuring there was no escaping from those swiftly descending lips.

His kiss was angry and ruthless, and she knew he was punishing her for her docile acquiescence to a life plotted by others, and challenging her to discover life on her own. His lips commanded her to respond, even as they punished her for letting a side of herself go undiscovered. And then, suddenly, swiftly, savagely, her struggle was over and the discovery did begin. It was only a whisper at first, breaking through her half-angry, half-frightened resistance. The whisper became a breeze, and then a wind.

A door, a door deep inside herself that she had tried to push closed, was flung open with such intensity she feared her own destruction. Because everything she had ever known was gone; all past, all future, Madame Lasard, Douglas, her father, the wilderness on all sides of them—faded to nothingness. Replaced by a white heat, and a gone-wild heart, a searing sense of aliveness pounding through her veins that obliterated all else. And it was not destruction, she realised slowly and abstractly, but rebirth. For the second time in her life she soared free, entirely unfettered.

A nature as feral as that of a windborn eagle flowed out of her to greet the feral nature of the man who claimed fiery possession of her lips. She was deliciously caught up in some internal rapturous dance as she met him passion for passion, ecstasy for ecstasy, heartbeat for heartbeat. A slow, wondrous trembling began inside her, her body a melting inferno of sensations that climbed and climbed to a surrender that did not feel like a surrender at all, but like a victory.

A startled strangled sound broke behind her, and she felt his lips lifting from hers, and saw his fierce eyes scan the trees with dark warning. But the kiss and the mood it had created were over, a summer storm that passed with dark magnificence before it really began.

Aurora stared at Chance, making no move to break from his arms, her eyes wide on his. It was over and yet it would never end. Not even his first kiss of days ago had shaken her like this. She felt as though she wore his brand now, that it would sear her soul for all time. She would never be the same as she had been ten short minutes ago, her life altered in a way that could not be explained in a rational world of words and rules, and yet was understood by hearts. He had, with this kiss, released her from the bondage of a life which, only a short while ago, she had felt she was doomed to lead forever. He had awakened her, but now she was held in a different kind of bondage. A bondage to him—to a part of herself. Did he know that? Did he feel it with all the raw instinct with which she felt it? His eyes—hooded, unreadable, faintly derisive—told her nothing.

He shook his head slightly, as though to clear it of some unwanted cobweb, and his arms fell back to his sides.

'It might be nice if you offered to take the tent for Heather today,' he said. Save for an almost undiscernible thickness, his voice was all business. 'I came to ask you to help Scott replant the sod over the cookpit, though I imagine it's done now.'

'I imagine,' she said dully. How could he be like this? How could he pretend it had never happened when her life was never going to be the same? How the hell could he be thinking of a cookpit? Of Heather . . .

'Should I apologise?' he asked, the mocking in his voice reminding her of his scorn for what he felt was her false virtue.

But could she ask him to apologise? For what? For bringing an immature and sheltered girl, a sleeping princess, to a startled, joyous awareness of life? For giving her a moment when she owned the universe? When the stars and the sun and the moon had been hers? For giving her a wonderful confidence in herself and her attractiveness and her sexuality that he could never take back, no matter what he did now? Apologise?

'You'll never be a gentleman,' she said scathingly, 'so why bother?' She turned sharply on her heel and stomped away.

Lusty animal! Aurora thought furiously to herself. What kind of man was he? Just last night he had spent a romantic evening with Heather watching the sunset!

Had Heather been the recipient of one of those kisses? Is that why she had been so determined that she was in love? Love, indeed! Lust, lust, lust!

But, after that kiss, could she really brand Chance the only lusty animal? She had responded—responded with a fire and passion that, as startling as it might be, still had matched his. Chemistry, she concluded again. That was what the whole camp had either seen or sensed between them, long before she had seen it herself.

She was so lost in thought that she almost ran right into Heather. One look at the other woman's face, and Aurora knew sinkingly that this was the intruder who had witnessed that feral kiss.

'You did it just because I said I liked him,' Heather accused in a spite-filled hiss. 'I know women like you. You have to have everything! A man becomes more attractive when he belongs to another woman. It boosts your confidence, makes you feel more attractive yourself to be able to take him away!'

Aurora sensed that the raw anger Heather was radiating was not so much directed at her as at the woman who had taken her Don away, and she felt a surge of pity for the other girl.

'Heather,' she said quietly and firmly, 'I despise Chance Cody. It wasn't as it looked.' Though she would have been hard pressed to say what it *was* like.

Heather's face remained frozen and angry, and Aurora sighed. 'I'll take the tent today, if you want.'

'Fine,' Heather said coldly, turning her back abruptly and striding away.

A short while later, Aurora found the tent all rolled up and ready for her. She rearranged the things in her pack to fit the tent, swung it on to her back and determinedly pronounced herself ready for another day, trying to ignore the churning inside her stomach.

But she found that, once again, the magnificent and scenic country they were passing through was almost totally lost to her. She was again enshrouded in a fog of anguish, this time mental and emotional, where before it had been physical.

She had to stay away from Chance Cody, she thought. She had to build a barrier of ice around herself that those blazing black eyes would be incapable of melting.

The further she got away from that kiss, the more she was stunned by it. Stunned by the passion she was capable of; stunned by how easily that powerful man had drawn an uninhibited response from her; stunned by the craving lingering in her to feel his mouth again, his arms, his chest hard against hers. Every time she glanced up the line it seemed all she could see was Chance—the smooth grace of his walk, the wind ruffling his hair—mesmerising her and causing a shiver of anticipation, of fear, of delight to ripple through her.

I've got to get hold of myself, Aurora told herself desperately. What's happened to my reserve? To my sense of propriety? To my morals? Can two kisses—ten minutes in a man's arms—really wipe out a lifetime of adhering to convictions and conventions?

She disgusted herself. It was a pure animal drive that was eating away at her, and yet it was most certainly the most compelling force she had ever felt. At the same time that it made her ashamed, she could not dismiss the wonderful bubbling it aroused within her, the heightened awareness of her own aliveness.

Thank God she didn't love him! Then she would not be able to fight it at all. To love him would be to surrender blissfully and without remorse. To love him and to want him would be all right no matter what the world had to say about it, no matter how scandalised Madame Lasard, her father, her mother and Douglas, would be. But just to want him was wrong. The fact that she wanted him so badly when she knew it was wrong just made her despise herself more. Was she really willing to sacrifice her scruples, her pride, her sense of right and wrong, for a fleeting few hours of immeasurable pleasure in his arms?

Yes, a little voice screeched inside her. No! she screamed back with determination, and renewed her vow to stay away from Chance as much as it was humanly possible; to remove herself from the temptation he probably knew he posed, and would probably not hesitate to manipulate. He was in his mid-thirties and unmarried; he must have used his magnetism a hundred—a thousand—times before. It wasn't his first kiss. Chance Cody was neither a schoolboy nor a monk. How many women had he practised on, perfecting that skilful kiss until he became the expert he now was at coaxing reluctant passion to the surface? It would be absurd to believe that kiss was in anyway as special, as moving, to him as it had been to her. *He* certainly wouldn't be mulling it over right now, wouldn't be obsessed with it as she was.

Yes, she would have to stay away from him. Steel herself against the dangerous temptation of loving him, of letting yet another man use her toward his own ends, her feelings, her depth, her nature, treated as unimportant and trivial.

What am I talking about? she asked herself crisply. I am in no danger at all of loving Chance Cody. He's obnoxious, unreasonable, ruthless, cruel . . . and yet, all the time she was trying to convince herself, she was remembering flashes of sensitivity, remembering a magnificent beauty that she was positive she had seen at the core of his soul.

It was lunchtime before it pierced the fog of her whirling thoughts that her pack weighed too much, that a four-and-a-half-pound tent seemed to have doubled the weight she was carrying. It gave her no satisfaction that she had carried it almost effortlessly.

Glancing around to make sure nobody was paying any attention to her, Aurora moved her pack off a little distance, and took out the tent. She unrolled it, and didn't quite know whether to be amused or annoyed at the five or six fair-sized rocks that had been rolled up in it.

'All's fair in love and war, I guess,' she muttered to herself. She sensed, rather than heard, Chance behind her, and quickly pulled the tent over on itself so he couldn't see the rocks.

He glanced at her impatiently, and moved around her, a quick flick of his wrist exposing the rocks. He stood and looked at them, his expression at first vaguely puzzled, and then slowly turning angry. He stooped and hurtled the rocks into the undergrowth with a barely contained fury, but when he turned and looked at Aurora his face was controlled and impassive.

'Would you mind telling me what brought this on?' he asked icily.

'I have no idea,' she said, bristling under the faintly accusing note in his tone.

'Could it be you've been shoving your princess routine down Heather's throat?'

Aurora's mouth fell open. The unabashed audacity of the man! He knew Heather was responsible for the rocks, and still had the nerve to look for a way to blame her, and defend Heather!

'My princess routine!' she seethed, her voice acid. 'I think it had more to do with your Casanova routine!'

'My what?' he asked, his eyes narrowed to slits, his voice deep with danger.

'Don't you act the innocent, Chance Cody! Just last night you were romancing her with sunsets, and then this morning she saw you kissing me. How did you expect her to react? Miss Sweetness and Sunshine is jealous—though how anybody could think they care about you is beyond me! She happens to think I'm stealing you away from her. How's that for ridiculous?'

'Ridiculous,' he agreed blandly, looking thoughtfully over her shoulder. 'This type of thing——' he gestured at the tent—is the worst thing that can happen up here. It's bad for the group. It could cause rifts if people decide to take sides between you and Heather, and there's nothing that can strip the enjoyment from a trip as quickly as a camp divided against itself.'

Now he was worried about his precious group, she thought, fuming. Not a word of apology for jumping to the wrong conclusion! Not a word of sympathy for the fact that she had carried twenty pounds of additional weight all morning!

'Then for the sake of your beloved group, I suggest you go make up with your adoring lover.'

Chance Cody stiffened, the fury back in his face. For a moment, Aurora thought he was going to strike her, but then he thrust his fist-clenched hands into his pockets.

'Not that it's any of your business,' he bit out coldly, 'but there is not the remotest resemblance to anything romantic going on between Heather and I. She's lonely, Aurora, and confused and hurt. Right now, the last thing she needs in her life is complications. What she needs is sympathy, support and understanding.'

'All of which you've altruistically supplied,' Aurora spat out disdainfully. As if he was capable of being sympathetic, supportive and understanding!

'Her tentmate certainly hasn't!' he shot back coldly. 'Dammit, Aurora! Couldn't you see the sadness in her? Are you so wrapped up in yourself that you couldn't see how desperate she was to talk, to be listened to? Couldn't you see how desperate she was to be liked, even if she was acting the part of someone cynical, and hard and unhurtable? Didn't it occur to you how she envied you, and was intimidated by you? You come from a world she's only read about, a world she's probably enviously dreamt about belonging to as she flipped through the pages of *People*. Do you think she'd let you see that? But if, just once, you could have stepped down off your high horse, if just once you could have showed her you were human——'

'I'm surprised that three days of near collapse didn't prove to anyone interested that I was human,' Aurora rejoined haughtily. But even as the words came out of her mouth, she knew Chance had hit a home truth. She had known Heather was intimidated by her name since that first hostile reaction to her hearing it. She had known, and she had to admit she had liked it! Instead of doing anything to let Heather know she was just human, she had deliberately kept the barrier up between them. She recognised it now as insecurity—Heather was so much better than her at wilderness activities, that Aurora had needed to play out her role as somehow superior, even if it was only for her name. She hadn't really even done it consciously, and now she was aghast with herself—and equally aghast that Chance had spotted her game with such ease.

'No wonder you despise me,' she said softly, the words slipping out before she could stop them.

Chance looked startled, and the censure in his eyes died. 'I don't despise you.' He sighed. 'I don't know why I get so mad at you, Rory. I don't know what it is you do to me.'

And you don't know what it is you do to me, she answered him silently, and I hope you never will.

CHAPTER SEVEN

AURORA stretched languidly, sprawled out in the sun, feeling very much like a contented cat. A whole day, she thought gleefully, to do absolutely nothing. A whole day's respite from her problems. Her main problem, of course, was Mr Chance Cody, who had taken himself, Heather, Hank and Danny off to do some mountaineering.

Aurora considered Chance a problem, though barely two words had passed between them in as many days, because he created a constant and baffling turmoil within her. She tried to despise him, instead she craved his company. She tried to be wittily sophisticated in his presence and instead tripped over her tongue like a gauche sixteen-year-old any time he was within hearing range. She tried to ignore him and be indifferent, and yet her eyes were always seeking him out—and to add to her general sense of turmoil, *his* eyes were quite frequently resting on her.

Problem number two—the problem she had come here to solve, after all—was no longer a problem. She was hard pressed to pinpoint exactly when she had made a decision. All she knew was that suddenly it seemed absolutely ridiculous that she had ever felt there was a decision to be made. She would not—could not—ever marry Douglas. She could barely remember what he looked like, and the thought of marrying him filled her with revulsion, not directed at him so much as at herself. How could she have considered trading her very soul for the safety and security he offered and because it was expected of her? Besides, unfamiliar worlds didn't seem as threatening as they once had.

She did have a third problem now, and that was what she was going to do with her life. She could not return to the emptiness and hollow frivolity of her existence under her parents' roof, even if they would have her back.

With the sun warm on her face, Aurora contemplated her options. She wondered if she should try her hand at writing. It was the only subject at school she had ever excelled at, and the only one she had really been able to enjoy and become engrossed in.

A story about a spoiled young socialite's wilderness adventure might be a good starting point to launch a career. She frowned. Did she really want her name to sell a story, rather than her merit? A week ago, she realised, she wouldn't have hesitated to milk her name for clout. How could she feel like such a different person in the short span of seven days? How was it possible that she had learned more about herself and about life up here, than she had in sixteen years of formal schooling?

Aurora cocked her ear at the sound of voices floating down from the mountain. The climbers couldn't be seen but the voice signals they called to each other came crisply over the mild summer air.

Scott came and sat down heavily beside her, a pouty expression on his face.

Aurora looked at him with sympathy. 'How is your hand feeling today?'

'OK, but not good enough to get in a little

mountaineering,' Scott answered ruefully. He looked behind to Aurora thoughtfully. 'Funny about people isn't it? They never act in quite the way you expect.'

'Oh?'

'Like when I cut my hand yesterday. I would have expected Heather to be Johnny-on-the-spot—cool, collected, knowing what to do. Poor girl nearly fainted at the sight of blood, and you, who I had pegged as the one who would be panicky and hysterical, just whipped off your shirt, wrapped it around my hand, and had me lying down with my feet propped up before I knew what had happened to me.'

Aurora laughed. 'Thank Chance. He's been squeezing a few first-aid lectures in for Danny and me. I think I was so delighted that if I had to have hands-on experience in a wilderness crisis it came in the first aid rather than the bear department that I could have handled carrying out open-heart surgery with aplomb.'

'Chance's reaction was interesting, too,' Scott mused with apparent innocence.

Aurora stiffened. 'What do you mean?'

'Oh, just that when he saw you standing there in that charming thing——'

'Camisole,' she muttered, blushing.

'—he had his shirt off and wrapped around you in about six seconds. And then he glared at me as if he wanted to kill me. Personally, I thought you looked twice as sexy with a man's shirt swimming around you and hanging to your knees as you did in your perfectly respectable camisole.'

'I didn't notice Chance reacting like that,' Aurora lied with faked indifference. She most certainly had noticed his reaction, and quite delighted in it.

Scott nibbled on a long piece of grass. 'You've changed, Aurora,' he told her conversationally. 'No, maybe not so much changed as just become more natural. Like at first you seemed to think it was some sort of crime to be nice, and you gave the impression you were looking down your long, snooty nose at everyone, and that you were determined not to have a good time.'

Aurora was unoffended. 'That bad, eh?' she said wryly.

Scott grinned at her with brotherly affection. 'As I said, I don't think you've changed so much, as just become more confident about letting people see the real you. It's nice.' He hesitated. 'I hope you have people at home who appreciate you for what you are, Aurora.'

She noted his face showed genuine concern for her and she smiled. It felt wonderfully good to have people really care about her, especially when they weren't afraid to show it. Though it felt awkward for her, she suddenly knew she should show him back.

'You know, Scott, if I could I'd adopt you and Hank—and Danny—for brothers. That's what I'm going to miss the most—the feeling of family you boys have given me.'

Scott beamed with pleasure and Aurora was glad she had risked expressing her feelings. They drifted into companionable silence, each thinking their own thoughts.

Aurora was thinking about how fast the seven days had gone. Sometimes it seemed almost as if she had been here all her life, as if life before this—before Chance—didn't exist.

Now there were only seven days left. A lifetime ago

she would have been marrying Douglas in less than a week. The time, she wanted to shout, was going too fast. It was all going to be over too soon.

I love it, she acknowledged, gazing around her and taking in the white-capped mountains, the alpine meadow spread out before her, resplendent in purple fireweed, the creek gurgling happily in the distance.

I don't want to go, she thought, I feel something here I've never felt. I feel free. I feel sure of myself. I feel like a member of a team. And I do feel like a member of a family. She pondered that feeling of family. That feeling of acceptance. For the most part, her strengths were made the most of, and her weaknesses overlooked, or compensated for by the strengths of others. She sighed. Of course, the family theory only went so far. Her sisterly emotions certainly extended to Scott and Hank and Danny, but what she felt for Chance could never be described as sisterly.

But there was something else that had happened up here that had made her feel good. She, and everybody else, had started with a completely fresh slate. It didn't matter who they were or what they'd done on the 'outside'. Ex-convict and society girl had equal opportunities to prove the stuff they were really made of. The past was without relevance, money, status, or three cars and a yacht having absolutely no bearing on anything up here. Aurora's place, for the first time in her life, could not be won with her name, was not assured by her prestigious background. Her extremely well-polished manners, her well-practised small talk repertoire, exquisite clothing, and expensive jewellery meant nothing. The shell had been totally stripped away, and her acceptance was based on herself alone, a self left raw and real by the environment, by the everyday challenges and hardships, by an isolation that led to intense and honest interaction.

She fitted, she realised. With no pretensions, and no conscious effort on her part, she was accepted. She was discovering something wonderfully genuine, honest and deep in her nature that a week ago she had not realised existed. But now that she did know it existed, returning to her mother's and father's world of sad and shallow superficiality was going to be difficult, if not downright impossible!

She contemplated again the article she might write. If she used a pseudonym she could be sure her article would sell only on merit. Would it? She looked about her with appreciation and suddenly was eager to try and capture the spirit of her experience on paper.

She was abruptly shaken out of her plotting as Chance's voice broke from the others, and rang down the mountain. Panic rose in her throat, and she bolted to a sitting position, her eyes terror-filled on the now ominously silent mountain, her heart beating too rapidly, and her face drained of all colour.

'What is it, Aurora?' Scott shook Aurora's shoulder gently to break past her fear-induced trance.

Slowly, Aurora turned stricken eyes to him, and then back to the mountain.

'I heard Chance,' she managed to whisper. 'I heard Chance shout that he was falling.'

Scott squeezed her shoulder. 'Hey, it's nothing, Aurora. A voice signal that the climber gives to the belayer—to the person he's roped to—to warn him to brace himself because the foothold has been lost. In a minute, he'll have recovered from the fall, and you'll hear him call that he's climbing again.'

But it wasn't a minute. It was a lifetime that passed before she heard his voice again. Then, just as Scott had predicted, Chance called out 'climbing', his voice completely unperturbed.

Aurora buried her head in her hands, feeling faint with relief. For a terrible moment she had pictured that magnificent body shattered on some sharp-edged cliff; for a terrible moment all of her life seemed a waste because she hadn't told him, hadn't allowed herself the joy of——

She sensed the concerned eyes on her face, and slowly looked up, trying to smile, but not quite succeeding over the tears that trembled in her eyes.

Scott took in the pale face, and the shaking hands, a tiny, knowing smile on his lips. 'You love him,' he guessed softly.

The tears ached behind Aurora's lashes, and she looked again to the mountain. There was no sense in playing the game any more. She had been able to fool herself until just a few seconds ago. And then suddenly, and with all her heart and soul, she acknowledged the truth. It wasn't just the Yukon that she had fallen in love with. It wasn't just the peace and tranquillity of this great untamed wilderness.

It was Chance that she loved. It was Chance whom she'd loved from the moment she had first seen him walking across that clearing with that long, ground-eating stride, with all the grace and control of a lion. Chance with those black eyes—those devastating black eyes—that could stop a heart or make it begin to beat with painful rapidity. Chance who led them with calm and with competence, giving each of them a sense of his own capabilities, instilling in each member of his group a confidence that would transcend their two-week stay in the wilderness. Chance who could be fire and ice, Chance who could be all charm and charisma and, equally, all stern, no-nonsense authority. Chance who could be brooding and unreadable, Chance who could show glimpses of incredible depth and sensitivity. Chance—a mystery so great and so awesome it would take a lifetime to know him, and Chance whom she felt she had always known and always would know.

'Yes,' she whispered her answer. 'I love Chance.'

The admission was the most exhilarating and frightening surrender of her entire life.

That morning Aurora had actually offered to cook dinner for the returning climbers, and had been relieved that if anybody felt abject amazement over her offer they managed to keep it to themselves. Now, she was doubly glad she'd overcome her reservations about appearing obsequious or eager to win approval, for when the climbers returned she was immersed in her preparations, and scowling thoughtfully at a recipe. With nothing to do she might not have been able to resist the temptation to run to him and throw herself wantonly into his arms, her joy in his safety apparent in her face.

She did allow herself a small peep at him. She gave an inward sigh of pure appreciation at his solid strength, at the masculine, poetic beauty of him. He threw back his head and laughed at something Hank said, and her eyes caught on the powerful column of this throat, and the strong white flash of his teeth, before she forced herself to look away.

I could easily make a fool of myself for this man, she thought, and her spine stiffened. What if her love, for all her efforts, was shining out of her eyes for the whole world to see? Abruptly, without greeting the conquerers of the mountain or the conquerer of her heart, she turned back to her tasks.

It isn't real, she scolded herself blackly. It's only some arrested form of juvenile hero worship. Real people didn't fall in love in seven days! That kind of romantic drama was reserved for books and films. And even if it was real, what did it matter if he didn't love her back?

But then she made the mistake of glancing at him again. Her heart fell, with a thrilled thud, to the bottom of her belly, and she was torturously aware that loving Chance Cody was the most real experience of her entire life.

Dinner was a disaster, a fact that surprised Aurora very little since she knew, despite appearances, that her mind had been a million miles away. Still, she could have sworn she had followed the directions fairly accurately.

She took her ribbing good-naturedly, even a little pleased that nobody tried to soften the blow of her failure by saying things they didn't mean. Heather looked smug, but Aurora wasn't sure that was a bad thing. She was more than aware that the other woman felt more and more threatened by her own growing proficiency in various areas of wilderness survival. Heather was losing her edge in the only area that she had felt comfortably superior to Aurora, and Aurora surprised herself by actually understanding her tent-mate's resentment, even if she was baffled by how to attempt healing the rifts between them. She had made a few awkward efforts at extending the olive branch, but the incident with Scott's hand had set her back to square one.

Danny strolled over to where Aurora was cleaning up. 'Good dinner,' he teased, smacking his lips over the crackers and cheese he was munching.

'Beat it, or I'll throw something at you,' Aurora threatened.

Danny looked at his feet. 'I'm sorry about that.'

'Did I miss something? About what?'

Danny sneaked her a gauging look, then looked at his feet again. 'I came within a hair of throwing my dinner at you last night.'

'Did you?' Aurora was shocked. 'Why?'

'I couldn't believe anybody lived who didn't know what macaroni and cheese was, and who liked it to boot. I've eaten it just about every day of my life.'

'Have you? Why would you ever eat something you don't like, let alone every day?'

'It's cheap,' he said bitterly.

Aurora felt as if he had slapped her, and suddenly remembered the look of distressed anger he had given her last night, almost as though she had betrayed him. And now she felt almost as if she had. How had she managed to live in blissful ignorance of the fact that some people ate things they didn't like—if they ate at all? It wasn't that she hadn't known there were poor people, she admitted reluctantly; she simply hadn't cared. It was an abstract concept that had never touched her life before. Now that abstract concept had a face, a face that could look almost heartbreakingly angelic at times.

'I'm sorry,' she whispered, and Danny shrugged and looked uncomfortable. She lightened her tone. 'So, why didn't you throw it at me?'

Danny grinned sheepishly. 'I guess Chance saw it coming. He leaned over and told me that if I did, he'd break both my arms.'

'Trust Chance,' she muttered scornfully.

'Chance reads people pretty good. I guess he knew I'd reached a point where I wouldn't think things through. I would have tossed it at you—I might have been sorry later, but I still would have done it. I just get mad sometimes and don't think. Chance ain't so bad, I guess. He knows the score.' Danny's voice held grudging admiration.

The last thing Aurora needed at the moment was one more person singing Chance's praises. It only seemed to confirm the absolute sense of her own strong feelings for him.

She tossed a towel at Danny. 'Dry,' she orderd, pointing at the dishes.

'Deal,' he said with a relieved grin.

Out of the corner of her eye Aurora saw Chance sifting through the food supplies, and felt a terrible sense of failure; the poor man was probably starving to death. Except that he wasn't eating anything. He was sniffing the contents of the packages, tasting little samples off the tip of his finger, and looking blacker and blacker.

He moved away from the food with a purposeful

stride, his lips set in a firm, resolute line.

'What's that all about?' Aurora murmured, watching him approach Heather.

Danny, who had been watching the scene with interest, snapped his fingers. 'I think I know.'

She was sure he probably did. He had an amazingly quick mind. 'Well?' she demanded.

Danny watched Heather and Chance shrewdly. 'She's going to cry,' he predicted, and then added scornfully, 'aw, and he's going to buy it.'

Aurora looked over the clearing at them. Sure enough, Heather's face was tearfully screwed up, and Chance was putting a reassuring arm around her shoulders and guiding her into the privacy of the woods. Danny looked at Aurora.

'My guess is that she changed the labels in the food bags,' he told her. 'That's why everything tasted so yucky. You probably made hot chocolate with instant potatoes and biscuits with powdered milk. What a lousy trick to pull.' Danny started to laugh. 'Almost wish I would have thought of it myself.'

Actually, Aurora might have laughed, too, if she had thought the little stunt had been pulled out of mischief instead of malice.

'Who would you have pulled it on?' she asked Danny sternly.

'Chance,' Danny responded without hesitation, and then Aurora did laugh.

Chance re-emerged from the forest several minutes later. Heather was not with him. He made his way purposefully over to Aurora.

'We need to talk.'

If he accuses me of pulling my princess routine, I'll probably start crying, too, Aurora thought. She steeled herself for the blow. And it came—but not in the way she had expected.

'Rory, the situation between you and Heather has gone as far as I can let it go.'

She opened her mouth defensively, but his raised hand stopped her from speaking.

'I'm not assigning blame,' he said, almost gently. 'The situation up here can magnify personality differences to intolerable proportions. I do a lot of groundwork trying to put together a compatible group, but . . .'

Aurora scanned his face for the accusation that she shouldn't be there, and she was prepared to admit he would be within his rights in making it. But there was no accusation in that handsome, solemn profile.

'. . . but it doesn't always work out that way, even when I've done my homework. Now, I have to step in and do something before the situation deteriorates even further. Do you understand?'

A lively little spirit was dancing in Aurora because he had avoided blaming her. 'I understand, *bwana*,' she responded, making her eyes huge and solemn. 'If you wish, just give me a pack of matches and a knife and cut me loose. I'll be fine.'

A hint of a smile touched his eyes and turned up the corners of his mouth and she felt herself melting under the warmth in his gaze.

'You might wish that was the solution,' he warned her, once again deadly serious.

'What are you going to do?' she asked, her merriment vanishing and being replaced by trepidation.

'I want you to understand it's standard procedure in situations like this. It's nothing personal. I'm going by the book.'

Aurora's trepidation increased and she nodded warily.

'I'm going to have to split you up. The twins have a three-man tent; we'll squeeze Danny in with them.'

For a moment she didn't understand what was so terrible about that, and then understanding exploded within her. Either Heather or herself would be taking Danny's place in Chance's tent.

It seemed for ever before he spoke again, and every nerve in Aurora's body was taut. It was a no-win situation if she had ever been in one: she couldn't go with him—not loving him the way she did—and if he chose Heather she would want to find a hole somewhere, crawl in it, and die.

'Aurora,' he said softly, and impersonally, 'you'll be coming with me.'

Aurora stared at him incredulously, trying to deny the relief that swept through her. He picked me, she thought with sad happiness, but now I have to tell him to pick again.

'It's no reflection on either of your characters,' Chance said softly. 'I made the decision only in the best interest of the group.'

'You should have picked Heather,' Aurora said, doodling in the dust with the toe of her boot. No personal preference, she told herself. It had been a decision made for the group. It didn't mean anything at all.

'Heather's at a very vulnerable point of her life. That decision would have been very bad for her—and very hard on me,' he said wryly.

And I won't be, Aurora thought, dully. 'Chance, you have to look at other options. I can't stay in a tent alone with you.' Afraid her desperate tone may have revealed too much, she continued in a businesslike voice, 'I'm an engaged woman. I won't have something like this putting a black mark on my reputation right now.'

'I assure you, your reputation will remain unsullied.' Was there a sarcastic emphasis on the word reputation? There was a wicked smile lighting his eyes. 'If that's what you really want,' he finished softly.

A shiver went up and down her spine. It was as if he could read her mind, as if he knew the real danger was not from himself at all, but from her.

'Chance, I don't know how you arrived at this decision, but it's ridiculous. I can't sleep with you——' A fiery blush lit her cheeks. 'I mean, I can't stay in the same tent with you. I think there are options you haven't looked at. I could stay with the twins——'

'No!' The word exploded out of him, and for a moment she was sure it was jealousy touched with protectiveness that flashed through midnight eyes. But the expression changed instantly, the eyes only mocking her fear of him. His voice was calm and patient.

'I don't think it would be fair to ask Scott and Hank to deal with the sexual tension of spending seven celibate nights trying to resist your considerable charms.'

'And if *you're* so completely indifferent to my charms, would you like to explain to me why you've kissed me?' Her voice was rising shrilly.

'If anybody has to suffer, Aurora, it's not going to be one of my paying clients ... And I never said I was indifferent to your charms,' he informed her silkily, his eyes half-lidded.

'You said I'd be safe with you!' she reminded him hotly.

'If you want to be,' he corrected her mildly. 'I'm not an inexperienced young man, princess. I can usually manage to control myself.'

'Usually?' she taunted, trying to hide her near-hysteria.

'Usually,' he agreed calmly, his eyes twinkling with devilish lights.

'I'll sleep outside, thank you,' she stated firmly.

'I'm afraid you won't, Aurora. A rainstorm would soak your sleeping bag, and wet down is as useless for warmth as a nylon windbreaker—and takes days to dry. If you're leery about sharing a tent with me, think about how much you'd hate being forced into the same sleeping bag until yours dried out.' He smiled as though he rather enjoyed that idea.

'Chance—please,' she whispered desperately.

'I'm sorry, Aurora.' The teasing, faintly wicked note was gone, and for the first time she heard the weariness in his voice. 'It's not an ideal solution, I know that. Unfortunately, it's the only one I've got.' He stretched mightily. 'I'll give you ten minutes of absolute privacy to get into your jammies, and pull the sleeping bag up around your chin.'

'Chance——'

'Aurora, I'm wiped out. Please, just go.'

She looked at him, and she could see the tiredness in that rugged face. She had never seen him look tired before, and she knew suddenly he really had wrestled with this decision, and taken it far more seriously than his teasing note let on. She felt an absurdly tender urge to reach up her fingers, and tenderly trace the planes of his face, as if her love could erase the uncharacteristic weariness she found there.

She turned from him abruptly. How strong am I? she asked herself sickly. She did not know if she was strong enough to resist Chance in these new and dangerously intimate circumstances.

CHAPTER EIGHT

HEATHER was in the tent when Aurora went to collect her belongings. She kept her face averted while Aurora quickly packed, which was just fine with Aurora—until she realised the other woman was crying.

'Heather?' she said tentatively, though her first instinct was to turn tail and run. She didn't have much time, and she didn't deal well with open displays of emotion. She had always been taught the decent thing to do was to keep your emotions to yourself. Never admit when you were hurt or sad; present that perfect smiling face to the world.

But suddenly that philosophy seemed perfectly indecent and callous. Was it so terrible for people to need each other? To need comfort and support and to seek it from another person? What was the alternative? To hide away your feelings with the help of a Valium prescription? To take pills in copious amounts, like Aurora knew her mother did, so you could give the illusion of being content and in control when inside you were falling apart?

Aurora reached across the chasm that separated hers and Heather's worlds. She touched the other girl's shoulder with all the compassion and understanding she was capable of.

'Heather, I'm sorry.' The words weren't so very hard to say. 'I realise I really shouldn't have been on this trip, and that you looked forward to it for a long time. My inexperience required sacrifices of you that you never should have been asked to make. It was——' these words were harder '—selfish and thoughtless of me to come, and if there's something I can do to make up for ruining——'

With a muffled wail, Heather turned sobbing into the comfort of Aurora's breast. Aurora held her helplessly.

'I'm sorry, too,' Heather finally said in a small voice. 'It was really childish. The rocks—and the labels. I'm not like that. Really, I'm not. But you just made me feel so mad. As if you had everything, and would always have everything, and had never known a moment's pain or longing in your life. And then Chance likes you better, too . . .'

'Shh. Chance doesn't even like me, let alone "better". He only picked me because he knew you had some things to sort out, and because if he has to share his tent with someone, he probably figured it would be safer to do it with someone he doesn't much care for.' Aurora sighed. 'And Heather, I've felt pain and longing, I was just taught never to let it show. Be unhappy but, dammit, be proud. There's a loneliness in that like nothing you'll ever know.'

Heather pulled slowly away, searched for a tissue. 'I'm just all mixed up, Aurora. I'm not usually mean or petty or spiteful. I think Don leaving made me kind of mad at the world. You didn't ruin the trip for me. I just wanted it to do more than it could do. I wanted it to heal me. And then when I saw Chance I wanted him to heal me. But it won't work. I still love him. I still love Don so God awful much it hurts. The way you love Chance.'

Aurora started to protest, but Heather ignored her.

'Want some advice?' Heather suddenly looked very tired and lonely. 'Run the other way.'

'That's exactly what I've been trying to do,' Aurora told her with a small, sad smile.

'Chance is right, Aurora. I do need some time to myself. I'm just too tense and on edge to be sharing a tent.' She smiled weakly. 'You do make a mess in the tent, but it wouldn't usually bug me—not as much. Little things bug me, maybe so I don't have to focus on the big things. That's what Chance said. Maybe a couple of days alone would help me get things into perspective.'

Chance! And ten minutes that were up ten minutes ago! Aurora bolted from the tent, but not before hastily assuring Heather she'd be available if she ever needed to talk.

Chance's tent was still empty, but Aurora nervously climbed into her sleeping bag fully dressed, removed her clothing and struggled into her nightshirt within the binding confines of the bag. She felt foolish over her safety measures when it became apparent Chance meant to give her plenty of leeway on the promised ten minutes.

Nearly half an hour passed before Chance slid in the door. He barely glanced at her. 'I thought you might be sleeping.'

'No,' she stated unnecessarily.

'Quit looking so distressed,' he ordered curtly, then added with dry sarcasm, 'I'm sorry, I looked everywhere but I couldn't locate a bolster to divide the tent in half.' Ignoring her, he pulled his shirt off, and Aurora squeezed her eyes shut.

How am I ever going to sleep, she asked herself with despair, knowing he's in here right beside me? She ordered herself not to reopen her eyes, but they mutinously opened anyway. She gasped to see him undoing his belt buckle.

She squeezed her eyes closed again. 'You're not taking off your trousers are you?' she asked in a strangled voice.

His voice was an odd mixture of amusement and impatience. 'I am. But there's nothing saying you have to watch.'

'As if I would watch!' she cried with outrage, her eyes flying open just as he peeled the faded denim off his legs.

A dark eyebrow arched at her, and he took in her deepening blush with amusement, and without a trace of embarrassment.

'Couldn't you sleep with your clothes on?' she demanded, her eyes safely shut again.

'I could not. If you don't want your sensibilities offended, princess, all you have to do is keep your eyes closed.'

She heard him sliding into his sleeping bag, and she knew he hadn't had time to put on pyjamas. 'Chance, you're not naked, are you?'

'As a jay,' he informed her wryly, not even a hint of apology in his voice.

I should have known, she thought frantically, that a man like Chance sleeps in the raw. 'I can't sleep in the same tent as a naked man,' she managed to squawk primly.

'Did you ever think you could walk a hundred and fifty miles, Rory?'

'No,' she admitted warily, not quite knowing what he was leading to.

'By the end of next week, you'll have walked nearly a hundred and fifty miles. So, you can do all sorts of things that you never thought you could do. Now go to sleep.'

His side of the tent grew silent, though she was desperately afraid to look at him and see if he was sleeping. She couldn't believe what she was feeling—a wicked awareness of the man who was beside her, a wild longing to turn and offer herself wantonly to him, to feel his lips, and the warmth of his naked skin against hers.

There was no escaping his presence in the tent, no matter how tightly she squeezed shut her eyes, no matter how hard she tried to force her wayward mind away from him. She risked a peep at him, and had to dig her nails into the palms of her hands to keep from freeing her arms from her sleeping bag and reaching for him. How gentle he looked with his eyes closed and his face relaxed, she thought, taking in the ridiculously long sweep of his eyelashes, the faint upward quirk of that firm mouth. She began to tremble with the effort of keeping her body perfectly still, of not giving in to its demand to move just an inch or two so that her sleeping bag encased body could touch his.

'Are you cold, Rory?'

She jumped at the sound of the deep voice. 'Yes,' she lied steadily.

Strong brown arms came out of the sleeping bag, and went around her, pulling her close into the curve of his chest, and she could feel the heat radiating from him. Oddly, the tension in her died and, with a contented little mew, she wriggled a bit closer. I'll never sleep now, she told herself defiantly, never in ... a ... million ...

She awoke with a start, so afraid she felt paralysed. Had she been dreaming of bears, or was there really something out there? The sound of her own heart pounding and her own breathing seemed to get in the way of her ears straining against the silence. It *was* a bear, she thought, fear drying her throat.

Chance's arms were still wrapped protectively around her, but she derived little comfort from the fact. How was he going to help when the bear ripped open their tent with one mighty swipe of a massive paw, grabbed her and dragged her off into the wilderness to eat her? Even Chance wouldn't be able to save her from that!

She tried to calm herself down, but she could still hear the noise that had awoken her. She knew it was the sound of a stalking bear, of his stealthy, deep breathing as he came closer and closer, sniffing out his prey. The sweat broke out over her lip, and her heart was racing frantically out of control.

I'm going to have a heart attack before the bear gets me, she thought plaintively. She willed herself to turn over under the weight of Chance's arm, and shook his bare shoulder with near-hysterical jerks.

'Chance,' she hissed, 'Chance, wake up!'

His eyes flicked open, and he looked at her sleepily through the tangle of his lashes. His eyes closed again. 'What?' he growled, his voice thick with sleep.

'There's a bear out there, Chance! There is!'

His eyes flicked open again, and narrowed, and, through the fabric of his sleeping bag, Aurora felt his muscles tense with alertness as he listened. Then she felt his muscles begin to relax again, and the alert eyes drifted to her face.

'There's no bear out there, Rory,' he told her softly, with insufferable confidence.

'There is so! Chance, I heard him.'

'Princess, I don't hear anything and, more important, I don't smell anything. There's no bear out there.'

Aurora propped herself up on her elbow and listened. 'I think he's gone now,' she conceded.

A tentative smile broke out on Chance's lips. 'What exactly did you hear, Rory?'

'Don't patronise me! I did hear him. I heard him breathing. Like this.' She imitated the sound she had heard as best she could, not caring if she did sound slightly ridiculous.

His smile widened and then became a gravelly chuckle. 'Not the most flattering description of what I sound like when I'm sleeping, but the bear really comes out in me when I've been rudely awakened.'

She stared at him, and then allowed herself a weak, abashed smile. 'Do you suppose——'

He met her gaze, his expression suddenly very serious and searching. 'You know, Rory, sometimes you remind me of a coyote. You make all kinds of intimidating noises, but you're timid. Underneath all that bluff and bravado, you're scared of everything.'

'I guess that's just the way I am,' she admitted. Oddly, she didn't feel attacked; in a way it was kind of nice that Chance noticed her enough to pick up on something subtle like that.

'I'll let you in on a little secret. There's very few things that are really frightening. You make reality inside your own head. Like tonight—your fear was real, but the bear wasn't. You created the fear. You created your own reality. Sometimes I think the only real power that we have—the only real control that we have in this world—is over ourselves and our perceptions.

'That's what I try and impress on the kids, like Danny, that I bring up here. They try to blame all their problems on the world, and they usually claim to be victims of circumstance. They don't feel any real power over their lives. If I don't teach them anything else, I sure try to teach them that they alone hold responsibility for their world, because they always have the power to choose their actions, behaviour, thoughts and feelings. By the end of the summer, with luck, they've glimpsed their own power, have begun to understand just how much they can do with their lives. They don't have to sit back and helplessly watch their lives being written for them.'

'How did you ever get interested in troubled kids in the first place?' Aurora asked.

He was silent for a minute. 'I guess,' he said softly, 'I wasn't very different from Danny at that age. Mixed up, angry, rebellious, and finally, I suppose, afraid.'

Aurora waited for him to go on, but he didn't and a long silence passed. He had just given her another piece of the puzzle, but this one didn't fit smoothly into place. This one just added to the mystery. Chance solid-as-a-rock Cody mixed up, angry, frightened? She listened, with regret, for the sound of his deep and regular breathing. It didn't come.

'Chance, are you still awake?' she finally asked tentatively.

'Yes.'

'I can't sleep. I got all keyed up feeling my real fear for a fake bear.'

'I'm kind of keyed up, too,' he said softly.

'Why?' She felt his black eyes resting wickedly on her face, and continued to look stubbornly at the roof of the tent.

'Because I want to kiss you,' he said quietly, and then added in a low, gravelly voice, 'I know of a great way for two consenting adults to pass the time when they can't sleep.'

She decided to ignore that. Not that she didn't want to be kissed, but she also wanted to savour the feeling of closeness she felt for him right now, not just physically, but in a different way. There was something beautifully intimate about whispering back and forth in husky voices deep in the night. It was an illusion, she thought, and even so it made her bolder than she might have been otherwise.

'Were you really like Danny? I mean, you were never in jail were you?'

'Yes, I was really like Danny—quite probably worse. And no, I never went to jail, though it wasn't because I didn't deserve to.'

'What did you deserve to go to jail for?' she prodded, shamelessly fascinated by the hint of a dark past.

'What is this? An inquisition?' She couldn't tell from his dry tone whether he was amused or annoyed.

'You know, it's not a crime to be curious,' she said defensively. 'And sometimes you can be a very mysterious man!'

'Mysterious?' Was his tone guarded? 'In what way?'

'Oh, I don't know,' she said crossly, beginning to feel sorry she'd allowed herself, in a moment's weakness, to let her interest in him show. 'I just think you're not just a wilderness guide.'

There was a long pause and when he spoke his voice was like silk. 'Is that important to you? That I be more than a guide?'

She sensed immediately that it was a loaded question, though she was afraid to ponder why it might be important to him that she accept him for exactly what he appeared to be. And she wasn't prepared to tell him the absolute truth—that she would love him no matter what he did because, no matter what he did, he would bring to it his inborn sense of dignity and grace.

She felt a stab of fear. Had she somehow revealed more about her feelings than she wanted to? Had those dark, frighteningly perceptive eyes barged through her guard?

'It really makes no difference to me if you're a garbage collector,' she stated coolly, her feigned indifference hard won. 'But I find it highly unlikely that Claire Bartek would have been engaged to a garbage collector—or a wilderness guide.'

She heard his sharply drawn intake of air and knew she'd succeeded in startling him.

'Danny,' he guessed almost to himself. 'I wonder where he dug up that little morsel?'

'Then it's true?'

'Hmm.' She assumed that was affirmative.

'She's very beautiful,' Aurora commented stiffly. My God, I'm jealous, she acknowledged unhappily.

'I haven't seen Claire for thirteen years.' Had he

sensed her jealousy? Would that explain the almost gentle note in his voice? Unexpectedly, he chuckled. 'It was the mis-match of the century. Or maybe it wasn't,' he added thoughtfully. 'As imcompatible as we were, we would place a poor second to my mother and father. Funny, isn't it, that I would almost make the identical mistake?'

Aurora held her breath, afraid to make a sound, in case he remembered she was there, a fact she was almost certain he'd forgotten.

'My father was a rancher—well-to-do in his own right, but not in the same league as the Ro—as my mother's family. She thought, given time, he'd come around to her way of life—globe-trotting, glittering parties and palatial homes, and he thought, given time, she'd come around to his—simplicity, hard work, fresh air. They thought what they felt for each other was enough.

'It wasn't. All time gave them was me, and enough bitterness to start the Third World War. The marriage dissolved before I had my first birthday.

'I grew up with one foot in both their worlds. I always felt ripped in two. I liked my father's world better. It was earthy and honest, challenging and demanding. It was a very physical kind of world, and I fitted there. I was always big and strong for my age, given to breaking the china at the birthday parties my mother was always arranging for me to attend.

'I guess I was just more like my father. Her world was always faintly foreign to me, and in a way she was, too. She tried to hide the fact she resented me, and never quite could. I discovered very early that I wasn't going to win her affection so I'd try for her attention. Every year my efforts would get a little wilder, and in the summer my long-suffering father would straighten me out with hardwork and discipline and then send me back to her. There were a number of brushes with the law, which my mother bought me out of. The fact that she did it to avoid embarrassment rather than out of affection wasn't lost on me.

'Years later, I came to understand that I hurt my mother. I'm the spitting image of my father, and I think I was a constant reminder to her of this great thing that couldn't be worked out, that destroyed itself in its own flame. You see, I don't think it was ever love they felt. It was a magnificent passion, but passion just isn't enough to get you through the rough spots.

'I learned that myself with Claire. I was still playing games when I met her. Still trying to win my mother's approval, still playing the role of the wealthy, somewhat wild, young playboy. But I was also finally growing up, and evaluating my life, and I realised I wasn't being very honest with myself about what I wanted and needed to be at peace with myself. I finally made some choices—a man's choices, made for myself, not for my mother or my father, or Claire.

'Claire was enraged by the choice I made, and that was very painful for me. I had finally taken off the mask, and the authentic person underneath was rejected— brutally. For her, if I walked away from all the symbols, the trappings and trimmings of wealth, I ceased to exist as a person of merit. And that was the end of our engagement, though it took a long time for me to see that it was a good thing—that for some bizarre reason I had attempted to repeat the mistake of my mother and father.'

'And your choice was to be a wilderness guide?'

'My choice was to be myself, and to quit pretending I was something I wasn't. My choice was to try and lead a meaningful existence, to change the world just a bit for my having walked here. Showing people this magnificent wilderness is a part of that choice, yes.'

'And the other part?'

'Nosy, nosy,' he chided, but then became serious. 'I'm the director of a large rehabilitation centre for native American—Indians, that is—who have drug and alcohol problems. As part of the counselling we do wilderness activities, as well as reintroducing people to their heritage, culture and roots. I sometimes think my great-grandfather is smiling down on me, and that makes me proud. I guess that's really important to me—feeling proud of what I do.'

It was then that Aurora knew just how different she was from Claire Bartek. Because instead of seeing Chance's choices as threatening, as foolhardy, she saw them as admirable and courageous. She shared his pride, feeling proud that he would insist on earning his own way, proud that his way of life—his soul—was not for sale, at any price. Not even for Claire Bartek's soft doe eyes.

She wondered if she had his kind of courage. She wondered why she felt her choices were oddly linked to his now. He had not, by word or allusion, committed himself to her in any way. And yet she sensed Chance Cody was a very private man, and what he had just revealed implied a certain trust in her, a certain respect, that he had never allowed her to see before. Was it ridiculous to feel that he was in some way testing her reaction? Ridiculous to feel that in some way he was asking her to join him in his adventure? Oh, he wasn't doing it with words, and yet she drank in the expression on his face, remembering that once she had wondered what it would feel like to see those dark unfathomable eyes become tender. They were tender now, and the tenderness was flecked with a smouldering light that caused a shiver to race up and down her spine. With slow gentleness he caught her to him and brought his mouth down to hers.

It was a natural kiss, neither ruthless nor punishing. It was a kiss that recognised the closeness that had been created between them by his sharing, and that recognised all that was the same about them, dispelling the differences for being as unimportant as they were. It was a kiss that welcomed her, and coaxed her and promised her, and she was helpless to do anything but answer it in kind.

It had none of the explosiveness of those other kisses, though it had the same urgent, driving effect on her senses. But the passion within her this time was not the firecracker variety, that went up, sizzled with vibrant colour and then was gone. No, this time the passion seemed to rise out of the very earth, rainbow coloured, and pine-scented, and as old—as inevitable—as time.

She recognised that something as ancient as the mountains around them had been born into her—a calling to discover her place in nature's pattern, a calling to discover all the mystery that lay within her, a calling to become a woman and to see how woman was made to bond together with man. This man. This man who had claimed her heart and soul ...

Vaguely, she heard her sleeping bag zipper being pulled down, and then his, and then she felt the satiny beauty of his naked skin against her, felt the dazzling fulfilment of featherlight hands exploring her with tenderness, and reverence, taking from her with a fluid movement the thin barrier of her nightshirt.

She reached for him, her hands as light as his own, her joy flowing through her fingertips, through her shining eyes, through the lips that could not get enough of his.

With each exploratory touch, with the deepening passion of his mouth on hers, the sensations within her intensified; the hidden delights her body was capable of were almost unbearable. Her body was entirely caught up in the creation of a primal, overwhelmingly beautiful symphony, the harmony of two bodies meeting to the wild beat of racing hearts and ragged breath, all her senses dancing and singing as his hands stroked her and lifted her high, higher, higher yet ...

His hand moved, tracing the velvet of her inner thigh, and a convulsive, delight-filled shudder racked her and then was gone as a vague shadowy fear pierced the haze of mindless ecstasy.

'What?' he asked in a husky voice, and she was reassured by his sensitivity to a tremble that differed from her other trembling.

'I'm just a little scared, Chance,' she murmured, her eyes wide and trusting on his face.

His hands shifted, moving to her face and tracing delicate patterns on her cheeks. His eyes were puzzled and searching.

'Aurora,' he whispered incredulously, understanding dawning in his eyes, 'Aurora, haven't you ever——?'

'No,' she admitted in a fearful whisper, puzzled by the darkening of his eyes, the sudden stiffening of his face, the reappearance of the sternness in the line of his mouth. His hands dropped from her, and he cursed under his breath. His face was a battleground of emotion—anger, bafflement, and something she couldn't quite define. Protectiveness? Wistfulness? Or was she just seeing something she needed very badly to see?

He started to move away from her, and she put a restraining hand on his arm.

'Don't,' she pleaded.

He looked at her hand, his face so glacial that she dropped her arm, feeling frozen out by his eyes.

'Chance, don't!' She was starting to cry. 'You're making it ugly.'

His hand moved, as if he would brush away the tears, and then dropped abruptly. 'It is ugly,' he said with strained patience, sounding horribly like a bored schoolmaster outlining the facts of life to an infatuated pupil. 'It's very ugly for an experienced man to seduce a raw virgin, to take advantage of the fact she's a long way from home in a situation that's taken her off guard and lowered her defences.'

'Chance, please don't! Don't make it sound as if I would have reacted the same way to anyone under these circumstances. It's you——' She paused, but the remote anger in his face made her afraid to say those final words. Afraid that to say 'I love you' would only confirm his suspicion that she was a naïve young girl, ready and ripe for passion, and eager to pass off her readiness under the guise of love.

Chance untangled himself from the sleeping bag, and tugged on his trousers. Without looking at her he threw open the tent door and was gone.

Swift anger replaced her uncertainty. How dared he arbitrarily make a decision for her, decide what was best for her? Did he think she was a child, or a fool, or both? Stormily, Aurora put on her own clothes, and followed him out. It must have been three or four in the morning, but it was broad daylight in the land of the midnight sun.

He was standing not far from the tent, his chest still rising and falling rapidly, and she went up beside him, the storm fading in her at the look of self-disgust she saw on his face.

'Chance,' she said, touching his arm, 'come back to bed. I know what I'm doing.'

He jerked away from her touch, whirled and looked down at her, his face dark with fury. He grabbed her hand roughly, looked down at the winking engagement ring pointedly, then let his blazing eyes drift back up to her face.

'Don't you think I know now? How much you must love and cherish him to save this gentle gift for him? What kind of man do you think I am that I would rob another man of his bride's gift to him? Do you really think I could take the passion that belongs to him, that's been building for him, and ever look at myself again? Now that I think about it, there were plenty of signs... I damn near hate myself for not recognising it was a yearning for passionate fulfilment in you that I saw in your eyes, and in the way you moved. I thought it an appetite for something you had already tasted, not for forbidden fruit.'

'Chance, please listen to me,' she pleaded. 'I feel nothing for Douglas. I guess I never have. The engagement is over. That's why I came here, because I was afraid my father was going to force me to marry a man I didn't love. I know it seemed spoiled and selfish to come on a trip I wasn't prepared for, but I couldn't think of anything else—of anywhere else where my father couldn't find me and bring me back. I don't want to be like your mother, or mine ... or like Claire Bartek. I don't want to be held prisoner of my name and my social position! Chance, I was supposed to be marrying Douglas on Saturday...' Angrily she twisted the ring off her finger, and threw it uncaringly into the bush. 'I'm never marrying him. Never!'

Chance looked at her, his face a mask, and then he gazed thoughtfully and silently after the ring. 'It doesn't matter, Aurora,' he finally said wearily. 'You just showed how useless it is. You just threw away a ring worth more money than I make in a month without even blinking an eye. You didn't blink, and I winced, thinking of all the people who are hungry, or struggling from pay cheque to pay cheque. If you had tried, you couldn't have come up with a better way to underline the differences between us and the choices we've made in life-style.'

She was momentarily wounded but she looked at him gaugingly. 'You know what I think, Chance Cody? I think you *want* to see the differences. I think you want me to be like Claire so you can run the other way. I think because of the example your parents set, and because you came close to repeating it once, there's one challenge you avoid, one risk the bold and brave Chance Cody has never taken. You've never risked caring about anybody, have you, Chance? Not in an intimate and personal way where you'd leave yourself open to being hurt——'

'Aurora, leave me alone,' he ordered wearily. 'Go to bed.'

Wordlessly, her back stiff with pride, she turned and left him. Back in the tent she let the hurt and mortified tears flow. She felt bruised beyond belief—by him for rejecting her, by herself for trying to force him to accept that one last challenge, the challenge of loving. Wasn't that assuming too much? Wasn't that assuming things she had no right to assume?

Maybe it wasn't love in general he was rejecting, but her in particular.

To his credit, he had refused to use her. He had seen, in something saved, the devastating effect a one-night stand would have had on her. How many men would have, or could have, turned from what she had so eagerly offered? How many men would have just given into the temptation, murmuring lies to be brushed off at morning's light?

Aurora sighed with weary frustration. To her discredit, she wasn't entirely sure she appreciated his sensitivity, his honour. It seemed to her that maybe one stolen moment with Chance Cody might have been worth all the pain that was its price tag.

CHAPTER NINE

'AURORA, I want to talk to you.'

'So talk,' she said with a shrug, noting with grim satisfaction that in the bright morning light Chance looked as haggard as she felt.

'Privately,' he hissed, strong fingers biting into her arm with an unintentional strength that made her wince. He let go of her arm, brief apology in his eyes, then spun away from her. Composing her features into what she could only hope was icy indifference, she followed him.

Finally satisfied that they were well out of earshot of anyone else, he turned back to her, studied her silently for a moment, then spoke.

'I owe you an apology.'

She raised an eyebrow, being deliberately obtuse and refusing to make it easy for him.

He went on firmly, obviously determined to say what he had planned, with or without any co-operation from her.

'Rory——' his unconscious use of the nickname warmed her slightly '—I misjudged you, and not just last night. And then, instead of being man enough to admit an error, I tried to lay it back on your lap, adding insult to injury. I'm sorry and I'll try not to do it again.'

Her admiration for him grew. It took a big man to admit a mistake. But the question now was, was Chance big enough to push beyond the mistake, or would he leave it at that, an uncomfortable stalemate?

'We've just managed to diffuse one unpleasant situation, between you and Heather. I'm hoping last night won't be the beginning of a brand new set of tensions.'

Her suspicion was immediate. Was that his sole motivation in apologising? To protect the morale of his precious group? Or did he really know how deeply he had cut her and was he genuinely sorry?

'I don't think,' he continued softly. 'It would be a very good idea for us to go on sharing a tent.'

Well, there it was. He was going to admit error, and in a backhanded fashion admit his attraction to her, but he was going to go no further. He was not going to involve himself in any situation where he might have to acknowledge that the attraction was more than physical. He was not going to involve himself in a situation that, by its very intimacy, would underline their likenesses and draw them closer and closer together, filling a need, an aching emptiness that Aurora had not realised existed in her until she met Chance, and that she sensed intuitively also existed in him.

She was coming to understand just how much they had in common. They came from the same kind of background, and though her disillusionment with that world was just dawning, she knew it equalled his. Douglas had provided a catalyst to her burning need for more, a need Chance had articulated so well last night. A need to rise above the superficial, to escape the gilded confines of a world that caged her with its constant emphasis on protocol and convention, that in some way tried to force people to become cardboard cut-outs, one-dimensional; dull and totally interchangeable with each other. A world that had not encouraged her to be strong and spirited, and probably would not accept her that way.

Cages. They came in different sizes and disguises, but love didn't have to be one of them. Couldn't Chance see that? Two hearts could soar as free as one, tamed only by each other.

How could she show him? Or was it assuming too much to think she knew something of his heart that he did not? Then she remembered the brief look of infinite tenderness she had seen in his eyes last night. No, she knew. She knew this man's heart ...

'Where are you going to sleep?' Could that casual, unconcerned voice be hers? But she knew you did not approach a wild thing too eagerly, or too loudly, but on silent feet, with an outstretched hand, waiting ... for it to bolt, or for it to draw nearer.

'I'll manage.'

'I hope it rains,' she said softly, tensing out of fear that she had said too much, told him too much. She waited, with her heart hammering in her throat, for him to bolt.

Instead, he stood very still, an unfathomable light flickering across stony features. He reached out, almost against his will, and traced the line of her cheekbone.

'You're playing with fire,' he cautioned, but gently. Ever so gently.

'I know,' she answered back. Gently. Ever so gently.

It didn't rain. And strangely it didn't matter. Over the next few days the group solidified into a strong and confident team. Aurora found herself having the time of her life. She rose eagerly and easily to the challenges of each day. She felt healthy and strong and happy. Coupled with the heady sensation of pushing herself to her physical limits were moments of tranquillity as she had never known. Plus there was a closeness, a camaraderie, within the group that was like nothing she had ever known. She was feeling emotions—joy and wonder and love—with an intensity that was almost physical, it was so gripping.

Her nature seemed to bubble like freshly opened champagne, and she knew a great deal of that had to do with the new kind of relationship she shared with Chance. He was as good as his word and, by unspoken pact, they had begun again. Each of them conquered the preconceived notions that had held them apart, and antagonism gave way to friendship as they tentatively explored their common ground.

The friendship deepened with breathtaking rapidness, as if each of them was anxious to make up for wasted and lost time. They discovered that they laughed at the same things, appreciated the same things, were moved by the same things. They found the silences between them were comfortable, the talks went deep and were enormously satisfying.

In spare moments Chance began to gravitate toward Aurora. 'I want you to see something,' he'd say, and she was thrilled that, without seeming to notice it, Chance chose her more and more as the one he wanted to share his world with.

And underneath the growing comfort and trust they felt for each other, an unexplored dimension shivered and sparkled with sizzling promise.

It was in the intensity she glimpsed in his eyes in unguarded moments. It was in the way they would 'accidentally' brush arms or shoulders or hands, the contact lingering until it seemed impossible to fight, and then one of them would back reluctantly away.

Aurora was aware of the clock ticking ruthlessly. But she was also aware it would be a mistake to try and force him, to try and capture him. It was one thing to tame, but to use the passion of his nature to try and cage him would be a crime. She yearned to know him more fully, to once again know the feel of his lips, his satiny skin against hers, yet she fought that yearning for all she was worth. Pure passion would be a prison, as it had been for his parents. It would not be enough.

And, though she was aware of the ticking of the clock, she felt oddly detached from it. In her deepest heart she knew, with absolute and irrational certainty, that she loved Chance and that he loved her.

Plus, she felt a growing oneness with the universe, a growing awareness of unalterable patterns that were a part of it. How could one face the glory of craggy mountains and fragile and intricate wild flowers placed side by side, and not somehow be convinced of an immense and magnificent life force? Become convinced of your own place in the world? It was a conviction accompanied by a feeling of all being right, and all unfolding as it should, and according to plan, without any effort by mere mortals to manipulate their own puny destinies.

Deep inside her, she just knew everything would be all right. Between her and Chance, between her and life. It was an odd irony, really—she was learning to relinquish control and just let things be, and at the same time she had never felt such control over her life.

Probably, she mused, because she was discovering who she was. She was letting go of pretences and just being Aurora. Even with Chance—or maybe especially with Chance—she played no games. She didn't try to impress him, or win him, or buy him. She recognised love was only worthwhile if she could be loved wholly and completely for who she was—to be loved for something she pretended to be would be a monstrous sham.

'Aurora, come back. Are you writing a book inside that head of yours?'

Aurora blinked and pulled herself from her musings. They were all sprawled out around the fire after a rigorous day on the trail.

'No,' she said sheepishly, 'just thinking.'

'Me, too,' Heather groaned. 'Of a pepperoni pizza with extra anchovies'.

'I think I'd kill for a Big Mac right now,' Danny said wistfully.

Hank passed around a bag of peanuts. 'Pretend,' he suggested unsympathetically. 'To get back on topic, what did you write today, Aurora?'

She had made the mistake of scrounging the camp for paper and pens so that she could record some of her reflections while they were still fresh and powerful in her mind. But as soon as it became known she was writing, the pressure was put on her to share. She had finally given in, feeling embarrassed and vulnerable. To her genuine amazement the group had been wildly enthusiastic about her haphazard jottings and now it was a ritual for her to read something almost every night.

'I haven't written anything today,' Aurora lied. She certainly was not sharing the love poem to Chance with anyone, including him. She was good-naturedly booed.

'I did,' Danny announced impishly, and took a bedraggled sheet of paper from his pocket, and cleared his throat loudly.

His 'Ode to the Big City' soon had them screaming with laughter. Danny glared at them with mock indignation as he sombrely recited his yearning for the roar of cars and jets, smoke-filled bars, the weekly instalment of *Dynasty*.

Aurora looked at Chance with a new thrill of appreciation. Danny was blossoming under the guidance of that firm hand, the sullenness, the wariness, the hostility, slipping a little further from sight everyday.

Danny's 'Ode' prompted a discussion of what everybody missed the most.

'A hot bath,' Aurora finally said dreamily, 'and Henri.' Was Chance really scowling at her? 'That's my mother's masseur,' she explained hastily, 'and after a day like today I could really use a good rubdown. But there's lots of things I don't miss that I really thought I would. I don't miss the television or radio or telephone.'

'I miss my teddy bear,' Scott wailed, and Danny patted him on the back.

'It's OK, I miss my rubber duckie,' he confided in a stage whisper.

The banter continued, and Aurora noticed Chance slip away.

'Oh, well,' Heather said, 'in another two days we'll be

on our way back to all our creature comforts—and missing this.'

'And each other,' Scott added softly. The mood was suddenly serious, and more than a little sad.

Two days, Aurora thought, and a fist tightened around her heart and squeezed. She gazed after where Chance had disappeared. Was she just kidding herself? Was it only part of the magic that existed up here that had convinced her everything would be all right? That things would work out, just as they did in the fairytales? She felt suddenly weary, and unutterably naïve. It didn't look as if the prince was going to kiss the sleeping princess after all.

She felt an abrupt need to be alone, excused herself from the group, and wandered away.

'Aurora.'

She stopped in her tracks, turned towards the voice, and squinted into the trees.

'What?' she asked irritably. She didn't feel like being Chance's friend tonight. She didn't want to share yet one more precious moment with him that was destined to become a memory, a memory that she was beginning to supect was going to haunt her and hurt her for a long, long time. A memory so powerful it might keep her forever from having what other people would have—marriage and children and happiness.

'Come here. I have a present for you.'

Against her better judgment, she gave in and moved towards him. As soon as he saw she was coming he turned and followed a narrow path through the trees.

She caught up with him in a tiny glade and looked around it curiously. A small fire burned, with several cans of water heating over it.

'Where's my present?' she demanded.

'There.' He pointed a finger.

She stared at a dip in the ground, with a water-filled ground sheet pressed into it.

'It's very nice,' she said cautiously. 'What is it?'

Black eyes touched her face, laughter-filled. 'A hot bath.'

He cares, she thought, studying him. But enough? Or was this just a parting gift to a friend?

Her troubled emotions must have shown on her face. 'I thought you'd like it,' he said, puzzled, his finger tracing the faint down turn of her mouth.

She wanted to kiss that finger, to grab it gently in her teeth and nibble it. She turned away. 'I like it,' she murmured.

'Princess, what's wrong?'

'Nothing.' *I'm leaving in two days, and you have to ask what's wrong?*

'Well, enjoy your bath,' he said and turned away.

She realised she had hurt him, and she deliberately lightened her tone. 'I will—and don't you dare watch.'

'I won't.' He turned briefly back, watching her with amusement.

'Promise?' she asked narrowly.

'Scout's honour,' he proclaimed solemnly and turned away again.

'Were you ever a scout?' she called suspiciously after him.

'Nope,' he tossed back over his shoulder as he left the clearing.

Despite herself, she had to laugh. Swiftly she removed

her clothes, added the hot water from the fire and stepped into her tub. It was a mighty shallow tub, but the sensation was delicious all the same. Who would have ever guessed Aurora Fairhurst would have enjoyed a bath in a plastic-lined puddle? she mused.

But even her sheer and feminine enjoyment in her bath couldn't quite dispel the greyness that was washing over her. If he didn't say something soon she was going to have to accept the fact that he was never going to. That he was going to watch her walk back out of his life without protest.

The water was starting to cool and reluctantly she got out and dried herself, pulling on her camisole and panties. She had one arm in her shirt when his cry shattered the air.

'Aurora!'

She looked at him, incensed that he would invade her privacy, even if he had never been a boy scout! But then the almost painful note in his voice registered—the treble note of fear. In his face in that split second she saw everything she had waited to see. His overwhelming love was imprinted on oddly tortured features. He was not looking at her, she realised, but beyond her, and the hackles on the back of her neck rose as her heightened senses picked up a pungent and disagreeable odour. She already knew what she would see when she turned to follow his gaze.

It was a bear. Huge and cinnamon-coloured. It was close enough that its rank odour was gagging her, close enough to paralyse her with fear. Even her scream was frozen deep down inside her. She and the bear stared warily at each other, frozen in a nightmare.

Then she awoke. Chance was running towards them. She could hear the thunder of his footsteps. Forgetting his own rules, she thought abstractly, forgetting just to stand quietly until the bear made its move—charged or lost interest.

Her fear dissolved, replaced by a dreadful awareness of the peril Chance was putting himself in. He was getting closer.

She took action. Aurora stamped her foot and clapped her hands together. 'Scat!' she ordered authoriatively. 'Beat it, big guy.'

The bear looked at her with astonishment, hesitated, then turned and ambled away.

Her body was seized with violent tremors, and then she was being scooped up in powerful arms, cradled against a mighty chest that was trembling as violently as she was. Was he cold, she wondered blearily, was Chance cold? She peeked up at him. He was laughing! The insensitive brute was trembling with mirth!

His eyes scanned her outraged face. 'Rory—Rory, you just told a six-hundred-pound bear to scat!' he choked through laughter.

'And what the hell were you doing?' she snapped. 'Man attacks bear! How smart is that?' The love she thought she had seen in his face was gone. Maybe it had never been, she concluded wearily. Shock set in abruptly, and she couldn't stop herself. She pushed her nose into his chest and wept.

'Shh,' he crooned soothingly. 'Shh, princess. It's all right.' His arms tightened around her and he carried her easily over the rough ground.

'My clothes,' she sobbed.

'Never mind.' He opened the zipper of the tent, and deposited her gently on her sleeping bag. His hands moved over her, soothing away the tension in her knotted muscles.

'Don't, Chance,' she whispered without conviction.

'Pretend I'm Henri,' he suggested, kneading life and warmth into her shivering, numb limbs.

I can't,' she protested sleepily, her eyes suddenly leaden.

'Why not?'

'Because I don't love Henri.' She waited for him to bolt. Instead he said nothing, continuing to work life firmly and methodically into her now heavy limbs. She sighed contentedly and closed her eyes.

She woke up once during the night. Chance's arm was thrown protectively over her, his face was nestled into her hair.

In the morning he was gone.

Aurora escaped to her tent immediately after dinner the following night. She had spent the whole day feeling mortally embarrassed, and the feeling was not fading. She had told Chance Cody she loved him. The fact that it was in a moment of supreme weakness made it no less forgivable.

This morning, naïve fool that she was, and still warm from the remembrance of his arm around her in the night, and his breath stirring her hair, she had looked at him hopefully, thinking ...

Thinking what? she castigated herself sharply, pulling off her shirt and throwing it carelessly into the corner of the tent. Thinking he was going to look at her with that melting tenderness? Thinking dark eyes would tell her, again, what his lips would not? Thinking the brush with the bear might have startled him into awareness of his feelings? Thinking, dreaming, praying, hoping, that, somehow and some way, today he would let her know.

But there was nothing to know, she reminded herself, brushing her hair with angry strokes that made it throw bright sparks.

Chance had repeated the story of her telling a large bear to 'scat' with devilish delight. And that was it—a gentle teasing, and then he had immersed himself in the day. Oh, once or twice she thought she felt his eyes resting on her with something like longing smouldering in their dark depths, but then she was a foolish and highly imaginative young woman. Only a foolish and highly imaginative young woman would believe Chance Cody to be capable of the finer things, like love. As if he, that strong, predatory animal, could understand a woman's sensitivity, her need to feel treasured and cherished, her need for infinitely tender gestures and reassurances.

No, not Chance Cody! Not Chance Cody who, after dinner, had winked at her, excused himself from the group, and walked away whistling merrily. Sure, he was happy all of a sudden! He was getting rid of them—getting rid of her!

Today they had arrived back in the clearing that had been their starting point. Tomorrow, the chopper would fly in, drop down, pick them up and whisk them all back to the lives they had come from.

As if she could ever go home again, she thought

blackly. As if she could ever be satisfied with the dull and predictable existence she had once known and accepted because she knew nothing else. As if any of the rich, suave, polished men her father would be eyeing as suitors could ever take Chance's place in her heart.

Well, if nothing else, she thought woodenly, she knew now just how strong she could be. There was something about walking through a hundred and fifty miles of wilderness, something about facing bears and racing creeks and endless miles of rugged terrain, that made the challenges she would face when she broke away from her family seem almost laughable. She found it hard to believe that once, a lifetime ago, she had worried that she couldn't make it on her own. Worried whether life could be worth living without a huge wardrobe, and several cars, and exotic perfumes, and expensive jewellery. And yet, for the two most meaningful weeks of her life, she had not only survived without all life's trappings and trinkets, but flourished.

Two short weeks in the land of the midnight sun, and she knew herself to be strong, a survivor. She was intimately and confidently aware of an inner strength and a tenacity that would pull her through any challenge. She knew, simply, that she was going to make it. Not on the Fairhurst name, but on her own gutsiness and innovativeness and creativity and courage. Her life was her own; her ability to chose it for herself would be her only gift from Chance. That stupid bathtub didn't count, and she wasn't even going to think about what might have motivated him to do something that could be even remotely construed as romantic.

'Aurora.'

She stiffened at the familiar deep voice outside her tent.

'What?' she snapped uninvitingly.

'I'm coming in.'

'You are not! I'm not decent.' He ignored her protest, and she could hear the tent door zipper sliding up, and scrambled for her towel, which she clutched protectively to her bosom.

'I've seen you in that before,' he said of her scanty dress, mocking her belated attempt at modesty.

She twisted to look at him, ignoring the ache of hurt and desire and longing she felt as she watched him, his back to her as he calmly rezipped the entrance of the tent.

'Get out of here, Chance——' She stopped when he turned slowly to face her, bewildered by the expression in those dark eyes, an expression so tender it seemed to bring into the confines of the tent a ray of warm, golden sunshine that reached out to her and drenched her soul with brilliant dancing rays of joy.

Her eyes drifted down to his hand. In it was an intricately woven wreath of wild flowers, and her heart began to pound, its wild tempo threatening to obliterate reason.

Firmly she twisted around, her back to him, still clutching the towel to her. 'You're breaking your own rules, Chance,' she noted scornfully. 'According to you, it's practically the death penalty for picking flowers.'

'I suspect even the sternest of gods smiles when the rules are broken in aid of a noble cause,' Chance informed her blandly.

'So, what's the big occasion?' she demanded, still not

trusting herself to look at him.

'It's your wedding night,' he responded, his voice low and unreadable.

She closed her eyes against the sudden pain that threatened to crush her. How could he do this? How could he be so cruel? How could he remind her tonight that, but for chance, but for an uncharacteristic surge of boldness, she would have married Douglas today? And now, because of Chance, there would never be a wedding night for her. It was not possible to feel what she felt for him twice in one lifetime, nor was it possible to settle for less. She refused to open her eyes, even when she heard him moving, and sensed his body very close.

'Princess, when I saw that bear I knew. I knew that I was willing to die for you. It only follows that if I'm willing to die for you, I should also be willing to live for you.' He paused. 'Open your eyes, Aurora,' he commanded softly, an exquisite note of tenderness threaded through his voice.

Powerless not to obey that irresistible tone of voice, Aurora slowly and reluctantly opened her eyes.

They widened. Chance knelt, the muscled surface of his legs forming a V around hers. He had removed his shirt, and his chest was bare and golden in the muted light of the tent.

His eyes drank in her face, and she could feel the hope she had tried so hard to crush rushing through her, sending tingling electrical sensations racing through her veins. His eyes, always so guarded, hooded and hiding his soul from the world, suddenly seemed to be the windows on his heart.

Am I fooling myself again? she asked painfully, her

eyes riveted to that baffling expression that softened the hawk-like cast of his face. His eyes rested on her with tender wonder. He looked so sincere, so genuinely enchanted, so possessive, so proud.

Slowly, with graceful and silent ceremony, he lifted the bright ring of flowers and settled it on her burnished hair. He was smiling slightly, and his hands followed the cascading wave of red-brown silk down to her shoulders. His eyes returned to her face, awesomely solemn.

'With my love,' he said, his voice low and husky, as gentle as the night breeze stirring in the forest, 'I thee wed.'

She stared at him, her eyes wide and searching, and she knew with sudden certainty, and a slow wave of exhilaration, that Chance Cody's words were as solemn, as reverent, as binding, as any that had ever been spoken in a church. His vow was coming from the reaches of his soul, and needed not the validation of a minister, or peeling bells, or a congregation. His vow was made to himself and to her. He was making her a gift of his wild heart.

She opened her mouth to speak, and closed it when no words came out. Her eyes, huge and green, as solemn as his, grew bright with teardrop diamonds. She blinked, and they squeezed out, falling silent and glistening down her cheeks.

Chance bent his magnificent head, and kissed the tears tenderly from her cheeks. Aurora let go of the towel.

His eyes moved with slow and wondrous appreciation over the soft curves of her body. Then, with a harsh moan, he drew her to him.

'How I've wanted you,' he murmured huskily, as his lips trailed soft kisses over her tingling flesh. 'I could have fought it,' he confessed, 'if it was just this——' His hand brushed possessively over her breast. 'But it isn't. I want all of you, Aurora. I want to know you—your heart, your mind, your soul, your body. It's as if you promise to quench a burning thirst within me, and yet each time I drink of you the thirst just grows. Maybe given a lifetime ...'

In answer she found his lips and gave him all she was.

CHAPTER TEN

AURORA awoke in the circle of his arms, and lay very still, gazing at him, and savouring the warm glow of loving him and of being loved by him.

As if he sensed her eyes on him, his opened, and took her in with slow and rapturous wonder. An unconscious smile played around his lips, and he reached for her and pulled her to him, his lips claiming hers with fresh ardour.

Without warning he pulled away, listening, his eyebrows furrowing in an unconscious scowl.

'What?' she whispered, wrapping her arms around his neck in blatant invitation.

Gently he disengaged her arms. 'You'll hear it in a minute.' His eyes swept her once more, with regret, and then he threw aside the sleeping bag.

Then Aurora heard the distant beating of helicopter blades. 'Damn,' she exclaimed in a low voice.

He touched her cheek. 'My sentiments exactly. Aurora, listen to me—we don't have much time.'

'I want to stay,' she said stubbornly.

He sighed. 'We went over that last night, princess. You can't stay; you owe it to your family to let them know where you are. And the next group is too advanced for you, and I haven't laid in enough supplies for an extra person. And I can't leave. Not for a month, anyway.'

He cocked his head—the sound of the helicopter was growing more clear. 'Listen to me,' he said again, this time with some urgency. 'I know it's unfair. I know time is cheating us of all kinds of things that need to be said and clarified. I know it's going to be the hardest month either of us have ever lived. That's what I want you to remember, Aurora, that it seems new and fragile to me, too. That I'll be wondering, too, if you're changing your mind, if it wasn't just a moment of mountain magic, the spell of the Yukon, that gave you to me. But, Aurora, if what we feel is real, it'll survive this month, and maybe even be stronger for it. Believe me?'

She nodded uncertainly.

'Good girl,' he said, and the sombreness in his eyes faded. He gave her backside a quick slap. 'Now get a move on,' he ordered. He was into his clothes and out of the tent before she had time to properly stretch.

'I'll call you,' he said a short time later. His lips brushed hers, and his eyes lingered on her upturned face. Then he broke from her and strode away, shouting orders.

Aurora lifted her pack, slipped it on and moved toward the helicopter. Tears stung behind her lashes. Couldn't he at least have waited here with her until she actually left? Couldn't he at least have said he loved her?

'Meanest three words in the world, aren't they?' Heather threw a sympathetic arm over Aurora's shoulder.

Aurora blinked. 'What?'

'I'll call you.' Aurora blanched, and Heather added hastily, 'Oh, I don't mean he won't. It's just the waiting, being scared to go out or to move away from the phone.

It's like being suspended between life and death till that promised phone call happens.'

A new group was unloading from the chopper, and things became quite chaotic between ingoing and outgoing people and supplies.

'Come on, Aurora,' Scott yelled, holding out his hand to her. She dragged her eyes away from the petite, tanned blonde who was eyeing Chance with undisguised interest. She took Scott's hand and was pulled aboard.

Chance's eyes suddenly rested on her standing in the open door. He froze, immobile among all the activity around him. And then he lifted a hand, and smiled. Remember that smile, she ordered herself dully. She moved out of the doorway, and sank into a seat. She struggled to remember the smile, but the doubts began to assault her as Chance Cody grew smaller and smaller in the distance, and then was swallowed up by the wilderness.

I knew, she berated herself despairingly; I knew from the moment I saw him that his heart was untamable. How could I have believed that it would be me who would tame it? Timid Aurora Fairhurst, taking on a man like that? Polished, sophisticated Aurora Fairhurst appealing to that feral man? What foolish bit of ego had ever allowed her to think that a man like Chance Cody would ever see her as more than a novelty—a new challenge—a passing fancy? In a month he would have moved on . . .

No, she told herself firmly, he meant it. He meant it last night when he had crowned her with flowers, and taken her for his own. She knew he meant it. She knew he meant it for ever. She knew him! Even if she hadn't known him very long, she knew him!

But a voice of reason was drowning out the sound of her intuitive voice. You don't know him at all, it taunted her. How can you know a person in two weeks?

Do you really and truly know Chance well enough to know exactly what he meant? You've never seen him except here. Here where he's the hero, here where he's in his element. You've come to know Chance in an isolated world that doesn't exist; can you realistically know him under those circumstances? Have you forgotten the savage in him?

It was herself that she could not trust, she finally admitted with painful recrimination. Had she been so besotted with him that she might have read things into last night that weren't intended and weren't there?

But then the previous evening materialised in her mind's eye. Oh God, he had been so gentle and tender, patient and considerate. And how could she dismiss the look in his eyes this morning? She smiled, suddenly, remembering he had even predicted she would be assailed by doubts, reassured that he had reminded her he would be feeling the same things. And the month had barely begun ...

Not even unloading from the helicopter could chase away that final sweet image of Chance. She said her goodbyes to her friends, exchanged addresses and phone numbers, and promises, in a daze.

'Heather!'

The sharp cry cut through the farewell chatter, and drew Aurora from her thoughts. With sudden interest she watched a tall, muscular young man run across the tarmac towards them.

Heather turned slowly from Scott, her eyes widening incredulously at the man running towards them.

'Don?' she whispered. 'Donny!' she shrieked, and raced across the tarmac into his outstretched arms.

Aurora watched, a small smile on her lips. She could hear Don telling Heather he'd been waiting for three days, uncertain of when she would get in. She could hear him saying over and over again how sorry he was. She felt a renewed faith in happy endings following separations.

'Aurora.' Heather was moving toward her, Don in tow. 'I want you to met my husband, Don. Don, this is my friend,' she used the term with a certain shyness, 'Aurora Fairhurst.'

Don let out a whistle. 'Wow! The Fairhurst?'

It didn't take long to get back to the real world, Aurora thought wryly. But the girl who would have preened under the recognition of her name was gone, and she was glad.

'It's just Aurora,' she assured him, 'and I'm just one of the gang.'

'You sure are, Aurora,' Heather confirmed softly. 'You added so much to the trip. I'm really glad you were there.'

Impulsively, Aurora reached out, gave Heather a swift, hard hug, and then turned and walked rapidly away.

'Well, slay the fatted calf,' Franklin Fairhurst said sarcastically. 'The prodigal daughter has returned.'

Aurora, fresh from the shower, and wrapped in a cosy, quilted Chinese robe, spun from her dressing-room table, a tart comeback hovering on her lips. It died unspoken as she studied her father. Before her stood a tall, paunchy, balding man. Two weeks ago she would have found him intimidating, with his arms folded arrogantly over his chest, and that perpetual scowl creasing his forehead.

Now, the folded arms seemed defensive, as if he were protecting himself. And the scowl couldn't quite hide the worry in his eyes. With a start, she realised he was trying to hide his vulnerability from her. Hiding his feelings, as he had always hidden them; trapped within the conventions of his world. With a rush of sadness, she knew that, despite appearances, life had not always been easy for her father. In fact, to her, he looked unbearably lonely.

'Why don't you sit down, Dad?'

He looked surprised and then suspicious. Finally, he perched himself awkwardly on the foot of her bed. 'Well?' he demanded.

Aurora got up and sat down beside him, smiling faintly when he squirmed away.

'I don't bite,' she promised him.

Some of the rigidity left him. 'Neither do I,' he informed her, and then barked, 'Where have you been?'

Selecting words carefully she told him about where she had been and, to the best of her ability, why she had gone. It was important to her that he understand it was more than Douglas that drove her away, that she had reached a point in her life where she had to evaluate and choose for herself.

'I was only trying to protect you,' he said defensively. 'And I still will. Douglas and I have discussed this at some length, and he's quite willing——'

'No.' She felt frustrated. Hadn't he heard her at all?

'Aurora, be sensible! The world is full of men who will use you. Who will play on that romantic nature that makes you so blind to their real motives. Now Douglas may not be the most romantic match in the world, I'll give you that, but he'd never hurt you, and he'd be good to you. That was always my primary motivation; if it happened to be a sound arrangement for the corporation at the same time, that was just good business.'

She drew in a long breath. 'I fell in love with someone, Dad,' she told him gently. 'I won't ever be marrying Douglas.'

Her father paled. 'You see? You fall for every line that every opportunist gold-digger shells out! How can you be so gullible? Who is it this time? A penniless vagabond posing as a nature lover?'

'He's a wilderness guide,' Aurora said proudly.

'Good God in heaven!' her father ejaculated. 'I wonder what his price will be?'

'He won't have one,' Aurora responded firmly. 'He loves me.'

'He'll have one,' her father spat out grimly.

'Is it so inconceivable to you that somebody would love me? *Me?* For what I am?'

'Well, of course not,' her father said with uncomfortable haste. 'It's just that these fortune hunters can be so damnably clever.'

'Give me credit for having some sense. Please? I know I made that mistake once, but I wouldn't make the same one again.'

'Aurora, be realistic. There's nothing sensible about

marrying below your station. Be honest, could you really be happy living in poverty in a wigwam or some such awful thing, with squalling babies——' He stopped indignantly when Aurora started to laugh. 'What is so funny?'

'Well, he is part Indian——'

'God!' her father exploded. 'Have you lost your mind?'

'Only about an eighth—Indian, not the portion of my mind I've lost,' she crooned placatingly.

Franklin shook his head mournfully. 'You've always been such a stubborn girl.'

'I wonder where I got that from?'

For a moment—just a moment—her father looked pleased. 'Has he got a name?'

'Chance.'

'Chance? What kind of name is Chance? Oh, God. Oh, dear God!'

'He's really very respectable, Dad. He has a responsible job, and he's from a good family.'

'High up on the totem pole, are they?' he asked with snide snobbery. 'What does he do? And what is his family name?'

'No, Daddy, you are not running a security check on him.'

'Why ever not?'

'I'd prefer you to form an opinion of him when you meet him.'

'And when will I be so honoured?'

'In about a month.'

Franklin snorted. 'With any luck you'll have worked him out of your system by then—or he'll have worked you out of his. Meanwhile,' a devious gleam appeared in his eyes, 'I think you should meet with Douglas. It's only decent after the blow you dealt him.'

'I'm sure he was devastated,' she said drily, 'but yes, I'll meet with him.'

'Fine. Fine.' He was suddenly eager to be gone, and Aurora was amazed by his transparency. He had feverish plotting written all over his face; his next call would be to Douglas.

When she did call Douglas later that evening, she knew her father had beaten her to him. Douglas claimed business commitments would not allow him to see her for at least a week.

What had Dad said? she wondered. Probably something to the effect of 'Give her a week or two. Let the memory fade. Wait until she's bored and lonely and then, wham, Douglas, my boy, hit her with romance'.

The fact was that she was bored and lonely and restless. She was driving herself to distraction remembering each moment with Chance, imagining future moments. It was finally out of desperation that she began to go through the notes she had made on the trip.

Aurora felt eagerness well up in her. She did have a story to tell, a beautiful and magnificent story, and not just of the wilderness. She immersed herself in trying to capture that story and the moments of boredom and loneliness and restlessness became less frequent. And she also came to understand that if she and Chance were to build a life together it was important she have other interests. Total dependency would strangle him. It wouldn't be fair to him—or to the strong, sure self she had discovered in that wilderness—to cling helplessly to him, to drive him crazy with demands on his time. Their relationship would grow and flourish if they both entered it as strong, independent adults who cherished the time they spent together but didn't crush each other with demands.

The project she started to alleviate boredom soon became a passion. Somehow, she'd been lucky enough to stumble into what she wanted to do with her life. Something that she could continue to do as Chance's wife ... and, some day, as the mother of his children. Each day the story flowed out of her, and each day her sense of purpose grew.

Douglas called, and she almost resented giving up the time to have dinner with him, but fair was fair, and she did owe him that much.

He's such a stranger, she thought, seated across a candlelit table from him, and watching him twirl his wineglass between long, soft fingers.

'So,' he said brightly, 'your mother tells me all she hears all day is the steady rat-tat-tat of typewriter keys. Surely you're not pursuing a career as a typist?'

'Actually, no. I'm doing some writing.'

'Oh.' He made no attempt to hide his relief. 'Nice hobby, writing.'

'It's not a hobby. I intend to sell—er—some articles about my trip to the north.' That wasn't quite true, but the whole truth awed even her a little. She didn't want to share the dream with Douglas.

Douglas looked horrified. 'Sell ... articles?' he said weakly.

She nodded, and decided to get to the point of this meeting as quickly as possible. The manuscript was waiting and she was just at the part where ... She brought herself reluctantly back.

'I owe you an apology for leaving you at the altar, Douglas. That can't have been pleasant for you, and I'm sorry.'

Her bluntness obviously took him by surprise. 'I understand you had some things to work through,' he said uncomfortably. 'Naturally, I'm willing to forgive and forget. In fact——'

'No, Douglas.'

'Of course, I don't think I'd want you *selling* articles,' he said absently.

He wasn't listening to her. She didn't suppose he had ever listened to her.

'Douglas, you and I aren't ever getting married.' She enunciated each word carefully.

'Aurora, there's no need to burn your bridges. Perhaps you'll change your mind after your father——' He stopped uneasily.

'Tries to buy Chance off?' she finished quietly. 'I think my father's going to find himself in grave danger of having both his eyes blacked if he's foolish enough to underestimate Chance like that.'

Douglas shuddered. 'Is he a complete heathen?'

'My father?' Aurora asked innocently.

'No, of course not! This ... this guide person.'

'Chance has integrity, pride, grace and grit.'

'My, my,' Douglas said and gave her a patronising smile.

Her temper flared. 'You know, Douglas, right now I can't stand you.'

He looked shocked. 'There is no call to be rude, Aurora.'

Her temper vanished, and she found herself grinning. 'I think sometimes there is.'

He regarded her thoughtfully, and began to smile. She wondered if it was the first genuine smile she had seen from him.

'You've changed somehow, Aurora. A little—er—grit mixed with your grace, as well. It's not unattractive. In fact, it almost makes me like you better, though I can't say why.'

'Maybe because real people are more fun than paper dolls, Douglas.'

'And does this Chance love the real person?' he asked sceptically.

'Yes,' she said firmly.

His look was long and hard, and then he smiled. 'Your father said you were infatuated. I don't think I agree. I've always heard that people in love have an elusive quality that makes them more becoming; I don't think I ever believed it, until I saw you tonight.'

He raised his wineglass to her. 'I bow out of the arena, Aurora. To your every happiness.'

She raised her wineglass back. 'To grace and dignity, Douglas, of which you have more than your fair share.'

'Mr Fairhurst, there's a man out there who insists on seeing you.'

Franklin looked at his secretary with irritation. 'Does he have an appointment?'

'No, but——'

'Then tell him to go away. Make an appointment for

him if you think he warrants it, but right now. I'm extremely busy.'

'I realise that, and I tried to tell him, but, he's just not the kind of man you tell to go away.'

Franklin stared at his secretary with astonishment. In fifteen years of faithful service he had never seen Mrs Harriet look ruffled. She looked ruffled now.

'His name?'

'Cody. Mr Cody.'

Franklin frowned. 'Send him in, I suppose.' He sighed. Salesmen were getting so damnably aggressive. Imagine slipping by the security. Imagine intimidating Mrs Harriet.

He knew immediately he had made a mistake. The man who towered in his doorway was no salesman. He was a big man, an expensive sports jacket tailored perfectly to fit over massive shoulders. He had coupled the jacket with jeans, and carried the combination with a casual elegance few men could have managed. But it was something in that face that arrested Franklin Fairhurst—the cool confidence of command.

He bit back his less than welcoming opening, found himself rising and extending his hand. 'Mr Cody?'

'Chance Cody.'

The name rang a faint bell. It was unusual, and he had heard it somewhere recently. Then he knew. He sank back in his chair, and regarded the man steadily. He dismissed, immediately, everything he'd planned to say to this man. Franklin Fairhurst prided himself on being a critical and discerning judge of people. Occasionally one could not be bought—at any price. This was one of them. To offer would demean only himself, not Chance Cody.

'So,' he said slowly, 'you love my daughter.'

A flicker in that hard, impassive face—of what? Tenderness. And suddenly Franklin Fairhurst felt relief, and a surge of joy for the match his daughter had managed to make without him.

'Why don't you sit down and tell me about yourself?' he invited.

Aurora fastened the diamond clip earrings and made a face at herself in the mirror. Important dinner guests, her father had said on the phone. She could tell from the tone of his voice he was up to his old tricks, and she had accused him of as much.

'Matchmaking? Me?'

'A young man and his mother?' Aurora pressed. 'Come on, Dad. Am I about to be paraded like a piece of prize beef? His mother, for God's sake!'

'Aurora, humour me. You are still living in my house.'

'At your specific request!' she sputtered a reminder.

'Please?'

She could have sworn she heard a faint teasing note in that uncharacteristically wheedling tone. It intrigued her enough to say yes, though now, as she gave herself a last cursory look, she was regretting it.

She descended the stairs. Her father and an extremely elegant white-haired woman stood talking to each other in the marble foyer at the bottom of the staircase.

Aurora smiled her best social smile as she went forward. The woman turned and regarded her with a piercing look that seemed oddly familiar.

'Aurora, I'd like you to meet Madame Gillian Robards,' her father said with beaming pleasure.

Aurora's smile remained politely fixed, though her heart fell. Robards? To what lengths was her father capable of going to see his daughter matched with this woman's son? She gave an inward shudder at the thought. Well, she was as strong as he was, and she hoped he was ready for a battle royal.

'I'm so glad to meet you, Aurora.' There was something faintly sardonic about her mouth that also struck Aurora as being oddly familiar, though it didn't seem likely. The famous Madame Robards protected herself against even a whisper of publicity; Aurora had never so much as seen a picture of her. 'I understand you know my son. He's parking the car at the moment.'

Aurora looked at her blankly, then cast a puzzled look at her father. 'No, I'm afraid I've never had the pleasure of meeting your son.'

'I'm afraid you have.' The deep voice came from behind her as the front door clicked closed.

A shiver of delighted recognition ran up and down her spine and, Madame Robards forgotten, she whirled. For a moment she stood, unable to move, drinking in the wonderfully familiar rugged plains of his face, the hard, uncompromising line of his body.

'Chance,' she whispered, and then she was in his arms, laughing and crying, and covering his face with breathless kisses. 'You came. You're even early. You——' She looked into his eyes, intimately warm on her own face. 'You love me,' she concluded with wonder. 'You really love me.'

'Yes,' he said simply, though he didn't really have to

answer. The answer was so plain in his eyes. Reluctantly he pulled those eyes from her face, and looked over her shoulder at her father. 'If there's a place where we could have a few minutes alone together?'

'The den right down the hall. And you and I, Madame Robards, will retire to the library. My wife should be down in a moment. Perhaps a drink until she arrives?'

Chance closed the door behind him and scooped her up into his arms, raining kisses down on her, plundering her willing mouth, letting his hands rove lovingly over her.

'God, I missed you. I couldn't last the month, Aurora. I couldn't. I was nearly crazy for you, and not doing much good at my job, as Danny was kind enough to inform me, so I had a replacement brought in.' All this was said in between urgent little nips and kisses. 'Marry me. Tomorrow. For once in my adult life I'll even allow mother to use her influence for me and get us a special licence. I think she'd really like that—the renegade son finally accepting the fruits of her affluence.'

'Chance, I never guessed—I mean, Robards! Though maybe Danny's reference to the "famous" house should have clued me in. It's the most photographed house in America, isn't it?'

'Between you and me,' Chance said drily, 'it's a mausoleum.' He looked at her searchingly. 'I didn't reveal my mother's identity on purpose, Rory. Although, as we get older, a grudging affection is developing between us, we're two very separate people. I've carved out my own life. That's the life I'm asking you to join me in.'

He was looking at her intensely, and expectantly.

'Chance,' she said softly, 'don't you trust me enough to know it's the fact you've made your own way, and been your own man, that made me love you? I love you too much to ask you to change. You didn't sell your soul for that house or that name. Please believe that I wouldn't ask you to, now.'

'How is it you knew exactly what I needed to hear?' he growled.

'I guess because I'm just beginning to carve out my own way, and I know what I'll need to hear—that I'm loved for the effort, if not the result.' She hesitated, then walked over to the desk and picked up a large sheaf of papers. She handed them to him shyly. 'I'm trying to write a book, Chance. I wanted it to be ready as a wedding gift for you, but it isn't. I, er, wasn't exactly sure of the ending.'

Chance read the first line out loud. 'I'm not marrying Douglas Hartman.' He glanced up at her and, grinning wickedly, set the papers gently back down on the desk.

He reached for her and gathered her into his powerful embrace. 'Let's do some work on the ending,' he murmured huskily into her hair.

BETTY NEELS' 75th ROMANCE

"OFF WITH THE OLD LOVE"

Betty Neels has been delighting readers for the last 17 years with her romances. This 75th anniversary title is our tribute to a highly successful and outstandingly popular author.

'Off with the Old Love' is a love triangle set amongst the rigours of hospital life, something Betty Neels knows all about, as a former staff nurse. Undoubtedly a romance to touch any woman's heart.

Mills & Boon

Price: £1.50   Available: July 1987

Available from Boots, Martins, John Menzies, W. H. Smith, Woolworths, and other paperback stockists.

Mills & Boon

AND THEN HE KISSED HER...

This is the title of our new venture — an audio tape designed to help you become a successful Mills & Boon author!

In the past, those of you who asked us for advice on how to write for Mills & Boon have been supplied with brief printed guidelines. Our new tape expands on these and, by carefully chosen examples, shows you how to make your story come alive. And we think you'll enjoy listening to it.

You can still get the printed guidelines by writing to our Editorial Department. But, if you would like to have the tape, please send a cheque or postal order for £2.95 (which includes VAT and postage) to:

VAT REG. No. 232 4334 96

AND THEN HE KISSED HER...
To: Mills & Boon Reader Service, FREEPOST, P.O. Box 236, Croydon, Surrey CR9 9EL.

Please send me _____ copies of the audio tape. I enclose a cheque/postal order*, crossed and made payable to Mills & Boon Reader Service, for the sum of £_____ . *Please delete whichever is not applicable.

Signature _____

Name (BLOCK LETTERS) _____

Address _____
_____ Post Code _____

YOU MAY BE MAILED WITH OTHER OFFERS AS A RESULT OF THIS APPLICATION   ED1

ROMANCE

Variety is the spice of romance

Each month, Mills & Boon publish new romances. New stories about people falling in love. A world of variety in romance – from the best writers in the romantic world. Choose from these titles in June.

NIGHT OF THE CONDOR Sara Craven
FORCE FIELD Jane Donnelly
IF LOVE BE BLIND Emma Goldrick
AN ENGAGEMENT IS ANNOUNCED Claudia Jameson
KISS OF FIRE Charlotte Lamb
INTIMATE STRANGERS Sandra Marton
TANGLED HEARTS Carole Mortimer
HIGH-COUNTRY GOVERNESS Essie Summers
CHALLENGE Sophie Weston
ELDORADO Yvonne Whittal
*****SAVAGE AFFAIR** Margaret Mayo
*****TO TAME A WILD HEART** Quinn Wilder

On sale where you buy paperbacks. If you require further information or have any difficulty obtaining them, write to: Mills & Boon Reader Service, PO Box 236, Thornton Road, Croydon, Surrey CR9 3RU, England.

*These two titles are available *only* from Mills & Boon Reader Service.

Mills & Boon
the rose of romance

ROMANCE

Next month's romances from Mills & Boon

Each month, you can choose from a world of variety in romance with Mills & Boon. These are the new titles to look out for next month.

- **WHEN THE NIGHT GROWS COLD** Lindsay Armstrong
- **COUNTRY OF THE HEART** Robyn Donald
- **FOR ONE NIGHT** Penny Jordan
- **BELOVED DECEIVER** Flora Kidd
- **BURNING INHERITANCE** Anne Mather
- **TO TAME A WOLF** Anne McAllister
- **CARLISLE PRIDE** Leigh Michaels
- **A PROMISE KEPT** Annabel Murray
- **TRUE ENCHANTER** Susan Napier
- **A LINGERING MELODY** Patricia Wilson
- *** HIDDEN DEPTHS** Nicola West
- *** BITTER DECEPTION** Gwen Westwood
- *** LOOK AT MY HEART** Daphne Hope
- *** GOLDEN BAY** Gloria Bevan

Buy them from your usual paperback stockist, or write to: Mills & Boon Reader Service, P.O. Box 236, Thornton Rd, Croydon, Surrey CR9 3RU, England. Readers in Southern Africa — write to: Independent Book Services Pty, Postbag X3010, Randburg, 2125, S. Africa.

*These four titles are available *only* from Mills & Boon Reader Service.

Mills & Boon the rose of romance

LOVE KNOWS NO BOUNDARIES

An aircraft forced down at a Russian base twenty-five years ago.

A diplomat in the romantic Vienna of today.

A young woman whose life was changed by a story in a shabby green exercise book.

These form the background to a love story of spellbinding power and unforgettable poignancy.

A stirring romance from Evelyn Stewart Armstrong.

AVAILABLE IN JUNE, PRICE £2.25. W●RLDWIDE

Available from Boots, Martins, John Menzies, W H Smith, Woolworth's, and other paperback stockists.